BEYOND
THE STARS

BEYOND THE STARS

RAY CUMMINGS

WILDSIDE PRESS

BEYOND THE STARS

I

"CALLING FOR HELP!"

THERE IS A SAYING in the Service that when Liner 40 N runs late the whole world waits. It may be true enough; I suppose it is. But to me, as Commander 3 of Liner 40 N on that night in May, 1998, it was a particularly annoying truth.

For I was running late; at the Azores I was a good twenty-eight minutes behind where I should have been, and it hardly made things any easier for me to contemplate an impatient world awaiting me.

All the way from Madrid our port meter 8 had been giving trouble. Then at 15 W. I had no sooner left the coast than a surge of wind from the northwest had swung down upon us, and I lost a good eight minutes trying unsuccessfully to climb over it. A mood of ill-nature possessed me. I was just twenty-four years old, the youngest of the three commanders who alternated on successive flights of the 40 N; this was only my seventh circle since promotion from the small equatorial liner of the East, and running the famous 40 N late under the eyes of a disapproving world disgruntled me.

At Meridian 45 W. the connecting Director at New York called me up. The Northern Express, flying north on Meridian 74 W., was already at New York waiting for me. The Director wasn't very pleasant about it. If I held up the express in its flight over the Pole and down 106 E., every connection in the Eastern Hemisphere would be disarranged.

The mercurial screen on my desk glowed with its image of the director's reproving face.

"You can't expect McIleny to make up your lost time," he

told me. "Not on a night like this. The Bureau reports head winds for him all up to Baffin Land."

"I'm having a few head winds myself," I reported.

But I grinned, and he caught my grin, and smiled back at me.

"Do the best you can," he said. And disconnected.

I made no ocean stops; but the director at 55 was a fussy fellow. I was due to pass him at ten thousand feet, to clear the north-south lanes for the non-stop Polar freighters; and with this wind and the fog which was now upon me I knew I would receive a sharp rebuke from 55 if I passed too high.

A hum sounded at one of the dozen mercurial screens beside me. Director 55 already annoyed! But it was not he. The small rectangle of screen glowed with its formless silver blurs, took form and color. A girl's face, ash-blond hair wound around her forehead, her white throat, with the square neck of a pale-blue jacket showing. And her earnest azure eyes searching mine, lighting with recognition as on her own screen she caught my image. Alice!

My annoyance at the threatened director's call-down died. I seized my headphone, heard her voice.

"Len?"

"Yes, Alice."

"I've been trying to get you all the way from Greenwich. They wouldn't let me through, not until I told them it was important — I had to get you." She spoke fast against the moment when the Vocal Traffic Timer would cut her off. "Len, grandfather wants you to come up and see us. At once — when you're through with this circle. Will you?"

She saw the question on my lips.

"Don't ask me now — no time, now, Len. But it's important, and grandfather . . . do you know where I can find Jim? We want him too, you and Jim."

"He's in the Anglo-Detective Division, London Air Service, New York Branch."

"Yes, I know. But he's in the air tonight. How can I get him?" Her smile was whimsical. "When I asked for a tracer, the Timer over there told me to get the hell off the air. I guess he thought I wanted to find Jim just to tell him I loved him."

Her image blurred.

The Mid-Atlantic Timer's voice broke in. "Fifteen seconds. Last call."

"I'll get Jim," I said hastily. "Bring him with me. Soon as we can get there."

"Yes. We're waiting for you. And Len, you won't need to sleep first. You can sleep after you get here. And tell Jim —"

A click silenced her. The screen went dark.

What could she want of me? It was pleasant to have seen and heard from her, this granddaughter of old Dr. Weatherby. In the stress of getting my appointment and continuous examinations and tests between voyages, I had not seen Alice since leaving the Equatorial Run. Nor Jim Dunkirk either.

I went after him now. The tracers could not rebuff me as they did Alice. They found him at last — at 120°E., 85°N. He was coming up over the Pole, and down Baffin Bay making for New York. His jolly face, with its ever present grin and the shock of fiery red hair above it, glowed on my screen.

"Well, Len, say, it's great to see you!"

"Alice just called me — Alice Weatherby. Doc wants us both — you and me — something important. Wants to see us. You off at New York?"

"You bet," he grinned. "Had a chase down through Tibet; every cursed murderer thinks the grand idea is for him to swoop it for Lhasa and parts unknown. I have one here, now. When I get him in his airy cage I'm off duty for a while. Alice wants us?"

"Yes. I don't know what for. She didn't have a chance to —"

"Fifteen seconds. Last call."

"The infernal bedamned it is!" came Jim's belligerent voice.

"Last call, Liner 40 N — limit ninety seconds by general orders." The Timer was imperturbably impersonal.

But not Jimmy Dunkirk. "You cut me off," he roared. "I'll have the General Inspector tell you who you are in thirty seconds. This is Chief Dunkirk, Patrol Liner A 22, Anglo-Detective Division. I've got a murderer here — understand? A murderer! Important official business."

With the Timer cowed, Jimmy would have talked all night. But I was on duty.

"Good," I said. "I'll call you at your office after you get in."

"Old Weatherby wants us?"

"Yes. Off, Jim."

*****

IT WAS WELL TOWARD dawn when I hooked up with him; together we flew up the river, where on the Tappan Zee, at the northern borders of the city, Dr. Weatherby had his home.

Alice was under the landing stage when we descended in the hand lift.

"Len, Jim, I'm glad to see you." She gave each of us one of her cool white hands. "Grandfather is waiting to — Jim, let go of my hand; you're squeezing my fingers. That hurts!"

He flung it away. He had always done that with Alice, to devil her.

"Next time," she said soberly, "you bow to me. That's all."

He laughed gleefully. "Right. Sure, that's safer when you look so pretty."

She was indeed pretty. A tall, slender girl — an inch taller than Jim. Big, serious blue eyes she had, and that braided mass of ash-blond hair. She was dressed now in a pale blue jacket like a tunic, to her thighs, and long silver stockings beneath the China-silk trousers that flared above her knees.

She smiled at Jim. "I'd never take *you* seriously. Dolores says —"

Jim sobered. "Dolores."

"Dolores is waiting to see you both. She's very excited."

Dolores, the little sister of Alice. I never saw her without a pang. In this great age of science she is a pathetic example of what science cannot do.

Our wonderful, marvelous age of science! We pride ourselves on it. But this girl had been born blind, and she was one of those rare cases where all the learned surgeons of our learned world could not bring the light to her.

Jim called, "'Lo there, Dolores."

"Jimmy! Is that you? I'm so glad to see you!"

See him! There was, to me, a grim pathos in her conventional words.

"Len is here too, Dolores," Alice said gently.

"Len? Oh, how do you do, Len?" Her hand reached and touched my hair in recognition. Then she turned back to Jim. "I'm glad you're here, Jimmy. They told me you were coming."

He swept her up, whirled her through the air like a child, and set her gasping upon her feet.

"Well, well, how's my little friend Dolores, huh? Want to do that again? Come one!" He whirled her again and panted. "Getting too big . . . all grown up. Say, Len, she's prettier every day, isn't she?"

DR. WEATHERBY was seventy-five years old at this time when he sent for Jim and me. He met us on the lower terrace of his home. He was a squat, powerfully thick-set figure, with long ape-like arms and a thick back slightly humped.

His head was overlarge, made to seem larger by its great mass of iron-gray hair. His face, large of feature, was unlined, save by the marks of character stamped upon it. A kindly face it was, smiling with friendship, but always stern in repose.

"Well, my boys, you came promptly," he greeted us. "That's fine. Come in." His huge hands gripped us with a strength that made Jim pretend to wince and grin mockingly at Alice. "Come in. We'll sit in the garden upstairs."

He led us up the inclines through his rambling house and to its roof, where in the starlight we sat on leafy couches in a garden blooming with flowers, shrubs and coned ferns.

It was about an hour before dawn, cloudless, moonless — a brilliant firmament of gems strewn upon their purple velvet. Venus was rising now to be the morning star and herald the dawn; red Mars, lying opposite and low, glowed like the ashless end of a cigarro.

Below us over the parapet of roof was the crowded countryside, wan and still in the starlight, with the tread of river beyond — a river of silver with the blue-white lights of its boats skimming the surface. A few planes were overhead, the small local airline from Albany skimming past with a whir of its fans.

Dr. Weatherby chatted with us, rebuked me smilingly for running the 40 N late, and listened gravely, with occasional interested questions, to Jim's vivid account of his world chase after the murderer, while Dolores snuggled up against him, thrilled, and timidly held his hand.

"Well, well, you boys do have an interesting life. Youth coming forward. Youth can do anything — the world waits on youth."

"It did tonight," said Alice, with a sly glance at me.

I wondered what Dr. Weatherby wanted us for. He had not hinted at it. He had spoken of a morning meal, and then we must have some sleep.

Then, abruptly he said, "I should not have sent for you unless it was important. It is. The fact that I need you —" He stopped as suddenly as he had begun.

I don't know why a great tenseness should have fallen upon us all. But it did. I felt it. And in the ensuing silence little Dolores left Jim and crept to her grandfather, leaning against him.

I began, lamely, "We came, of course —"

DR. WEATHERBY was staring off at the stars moodily, with a look so far away I could have fancied he was gazing, not at the stars, but beyond them. And then he tore himself back, and smiled, lighting a cigarro, flipping the torch at me and asking me to step on it.

"I have so much to tell you," he said. "I hardly know how or where to begin. You know, of course, something of my life, my work.

"Leonard, and you, Jim, I believe you're familiar in a general way with what the physicists think of the atom? Radiant matter — these electro-rays that seem to solve everything and yet only add to the mystery?

"You know that savants would tell us that space is curved; so Einstein told us years ago? Well, *I* will tell you this. Tomorrow, after you have slept, I believe I can make clear to you the real construction of our material universe."

His hand checked us. "I have been working since 1970 along these lines. Alice recently has been helping me. And then Dolores —

"This child here, in the dark, it has been given her to see things denied to our science. Years and years ago a scientist proclaimed that *thoughts* themselves are a mere vibration, like light and heat and sound, and all these mysterious rays and flying electrons — electricity itself. They are all the same, though we name them differently."

He had been talking swiftly, but quietly. "Tell them, Dolores."

"A big open space," she said slowly. "Mountains and a broad valley. A cliffside. People there on a ledge. A young man and a young woman, very white and pale, with blood on the man's face. They were standing on a height, with a dark cavern behind them.

"Other people, or monsters down in the valley: something

vague but horrible as a nightmare with a nameless horror. And the man was calling, *Help*. Not the word. I could not hear that, but I knew. Calling to me. He keeps on calling. I can hear him so often. Calling to *me!*"

She said it so strangely. At once it seemed uncanny, weird, almost gruesome. A thrill very akin to fear ran over me. This was not science. But Dr. Weatherby's calm, precise voice was scientific enough.

"That was several years ago. We have found since that she is receiving thought-vibrations, not from here on Earth, not from the planets, or the stars, but from beyond the stars. The greater realms out there, suspected to exist for so long, which now I know and can prove to exist!"

His voice had risen in an excitement, an exaltation. He went on more swiftly, "But all that is nothing. I wanted you to come here and help me. Dolores has had thoughts from out there beyond the stars . . . and her own answering thoughts have been answered. Communication!

"Oh, I have guarded against delusion! I have sent messages through Dolores of scientific import, and been answered with scientific thoughts all beyond this child's comprehension. Communications with the great unknown — the infinity of distance un-fathomable.

"That started a year ago. Now I have done more. I have learned how to get there. I can transport myself, my girls and you! I am ready to make the journey now. That is why I want you, and need you. We are going. We want you to come with us, out beyond the stars!"

.

II

THE DEAD WHITE THING

"IN THE PLAN of the universe," said Dr. Weatherby, "we find a conception gigantic, infinite, and yet it all has a simplicity. I want most earnestly to have you understand me, Leonard and Jim."

He gazed at us with a gentle smile. We had had our morning meal, and had slept long and heavily, and now it was evening twilight. We sat in the big living room on the lower floor of the Weatherby home. Dolores, as before, cuddled against her grandfather's side. Alice busied about the house, but presently she joined us. Dr. Weatherby's manner was as earnest as his words. He added, looking at me, "I want to be very clear, Leonard. This thing that we are to do — this journey, in which if you will not join me I shall make alone —"

"By the infernal, you won't make it alone while I'm alive," Jim cried. "The detective service loses its best tracker, beginning right away!"

Dr. Weatherby held out his hand. "My boy!" He could say no more. And on Dolores's face was a radiance. Then Dr. Weatherby turned to me.

"And you, Leonard — will you go?"

The direct question startled me.

Would I go out there into eternity? Beyond the stars, into eternal time, and over space unfathomable, to encounter what now no human mind could grasp? But, like Jim, I was practically alone in the world and I was free to make any decision without fear of hurting others.

Nevertheless, to give up my commission, as youngest commander of the great 40 N, to disappear, lose all I had earned, gave me pause. To return, perhaps never. Wanderers beyond the stars! Was this not, perhaps, too bold a thing for human endeavor?

I heard my voice saying quietly, "Why, of course I'm going with you, Dr. Weatherby."

I was aware that Alice had come in to sit beside me, her cool white hand impulsively pressing mind. And Dolores was saying,

"Alice, they're going! Isn't that wonderful? We're all going just as soon as we can get ready!"

"A STRANGE SIMPLICITY," Dr. Weatherby was saying. "First, let me make this clear: when I say universe — the construction of our universe — I mean everything that exists, or has, or will exist, the smallest entity of our infinitesimal atomic world to the greatest conception of what may lie beyond the stars. Does that sound complicated? Let me say again, it is simple."

He leaned toward us, with his thick, strong hands gripped in his lap. "I want you to realize first that we are dealing with infinities. The human mind is so finite, so limited. You must cast off most of your instinctive methods of reasoning. You understand me?"

"We'll try," I said.

He nodded and went on.

"Conceive a void of nothingness. No space, no time, no material bodies. Just nothing. That was the beginning. Do not try to wonder *when* it was. A billion years ago . . . a billion billion. Not at all. You must not think of *when*, because *when* implies time. There was no *time*. There could be no time without material bodies to create movement and events. For time in itself is nothing but the measurement between events.

"We have then, a nothingness. A vortex. A whirlpool."

"A vortex of nothingness?" I exclaimed.

"Exactly. Why, back in the 1920's, Leonard, scientists recognized that the basic entities of matter were only whirlpools. They hoped then to find some fundamental substance, like ether. But there is none.

"A whirlpool, but its very motion, simulates substance. And, in the last analysis, that is all which exists — an apparent solidity. Divide anything, probe into anything, you find only a *motion* of something else smaller which is apparently real. But then take that smaller thing. Divide it. You find more empty spaces, more nothingness. And other yet smaller things in violent motion.

"Why, Leonard, don't you realize that's what puzzled scientists? From 1900 on, they puzzled over it. They found a solid bar of iron to be composed of molecules. They said: 'Oh yes, we understand. This solidity of iron is only apparent. It really consists of molecules of iron with empty spaces in between them, and the molecules are in motion.'

"But then, Leonard — this was way back — they suddenly found that the reality of the molecules was only apparent. It was just like the iron! Empty spaces, with atoms in motion. Ah, at last they had got to the bottom of it. Atoms.

"But then they found that an atom was no more a solidity than the molecule, or the iron bar. Still other spaces, with other vibrating particles. And fatuously they said: 'We have found electrons, revolving around a central nucleus.' But that meant nothing, and at last they began to realize it.

"Let your mind leap beyond all that, Leonard. It is too fatuous to think that each division of matter is the last, simply because you cannot make another division. Let's go back to that original vortex of nothingness. It created an apparent solidity, exactly as the vibrating molecules of iron create iron. That's clear, isn't it?"

"But," said Jim, "how small is this smallest vortex?"

Dr. Weatherby laughed. "It has no size. It is infinitely small. An abstract quality, beyond human conception. If you try to name its size, then no longer is it infinitely small. It is *not* the smallest vortex; there is no such thing. It is the infinitely small vortex, which is very different.

"Conceive, then, this vortex, which creates an apparently solid particle of matter. I call this particle an intime. This intime, in turn, with myriads of its fellows clustering about it, vibrating with empty nothingness between, creates another, larger entity — another apparently solid substance. And so on up to what we now call an electron."

"Well," I said, "between the intime and the electron, how many separate densities might there be?"

"An infinite number," he replied smilingly. "A number that cannot be conceived. Each has distinct characteristics, just as iron differs from lead or gold."

He paused a moment, but none of us said anything. "With

this conception," he went on, "we can build the definition that a material substance is a density of other substances. It maintains its separate existence by virtue of having around its exterior an emptiness greater than the emptiness of its interior. Think of that for a moment.

"The Earth itself is such a density. The space around it is greater than any of the spaces within its molecules, its atoms, its electrons — down to its finitely small intimes — to the ultimate nothingness of which it is composed.

"That is our Earth. It is in movement. And another density near it we call Venus, and another Mars, vibrating with a space between them. All our starry universe; you see, Leonard?"

My mind leaped with the thrill of it. The great vault of the heavens with its myriad whirling stars shrank before my far-flung imagination into a tiny space teeming with its agitated particles!

Dr. Weatherby added gently, "A fragment of iron is microscopically no different in structure from our starry universe. The distances between our heavenly bodies compared to the size of them are quite the same as the distances between electrons, or intimes, compared to their size. You get my point?"

"I do," Jim exclaimed. "What we call the sky would seem a solid mass of matter — like a fragment of iron — to some greater viewpoint?"

"Exactly. Our microscopes show nothing which is actually more solid than the sky itself. From here, on Earth, to the Milky Way is to us a tremendous distance. But suppose that we were so gigantic — so vast in comparative size — that we needed a powerful microscope even to perceive that space. What would we see? A multiplicity of vibrating particles! And without the microscope the whole space would seem solid. We could call it . . . well, say a grain of gold."

For a moment we were silent. There was to all this an awesome aspect. Yet its actual simplicity was overwhelming.

Dolores said timidly, "It seems strange that so simple a thing should have been unknown for so long."

"Not at all," said Dr. Weatherby. "The knowledge came step by step. It is only the final conception which seems so startling. To me it is the logical, inevitable conclusion. How could the facts be otherwise?

"Always, therefore, we have conceived ourselves and our

Earth to be some masterful dividing line between what is smaller and what is larger than ourselves. That is fatuous.

"We call the one our microscopic world. The other astronomical world. And we sit between them, puzzling over their difference! They are both one, and we are in them — a mere step of the ladder."

"It makes me feel very small," said Alice.

"Or large," I said. "According to the viewpoint."

I added to Dr. Weatherby, "I realize now why no size, no motion, no time, nor density can be absolute. Everything must be relative to something else."

"Exactly," he nodded.

Jim was puzzling. "This voyage we're going to make — beyond the stars. How are we going to make this trip? What in? By what method? By the nine airy demons, Dr. Weatherby, there's an awful lot you haven't told us yet!"

"Not so much," said Dr. Weatherby smilingly.

"Because," I interposed, "you don't need to know very much, Jim."

"We're going in a projectile," said Dolores. "At least they say it looks like a projectile."

"Like Mallen's Moon rocket of 1989," Jim exclaimed.

Dr. Weatherby shook his head. "The various anti-gravity methods devised so far would help us very little, except Elton's electronic neutralization of gravity. I use that principle merely in starting the flight. A trip to the Moon, such as Mallen's rocket made, had nothing in common with this journey of ours."

"They say Mallen is going himself next year — to Mars," Alice remarked.

"Let's see our projectile," Jim demanded.

"In a moment," Dr. Weatherby said. "There is, first, one conception I want to make sure you have grasped. Forget our Earth now. Forget yourself. Conceive the material universe to be a vast void in which various densities are whirling.

"From the infinitely small to the infinitely large, they are of every size and character. Yet all are inherently the same, merely apparently solid. I will ask you, Leonard, this space between the Earth and Mars — of what would you say it is composed?"

I hesitated. "Nothingness," I ventured finally.

"No!" he exclaimed warmly. "There is where you fail to grasp my fundamental conception. The void of space itself is a mass of particles, a mass of densities, of every possible size and character.

"The Earth is one; a wandering asteroid is another. And meteors, meteorites, are the particles of light, far flung everywhere through space. Other entities are again still smaller — call them intimes — down in size to infinity.

"Space then, you must realize, is not empty. The emptiness, the nothingness, is only the infinitely small. Ah, I see now that you begin to understand!"

I said slowly, "I'm imagining space as . . . as a jelly. Unsolid, because we ourselves are more solid, and it seems unsolid to us. But . . . if we were less dense, and larger . . . gigantic —" I stopped.

"That," said Dr. Weatherby, "is precisely the point of view I've wanted you to get. You can understand now why to beings of some greater outside realm all our interstellar space would shrink into apparent solidity, and they would call it an atom.

"CONCEIVE YOURSELF now a scientist of that vast universe outside. You are living on a density — a great conglomeration of particles clinging together — and you call it your Earth.

"One tiny particle of your Earth is beneath your microscope. You call it a grain of gold. You examine it. You find it is not solid. You see 'empty spaces.' They are not really empty, but the particles of matter swimming in them are too small for you to see. But you do see what you call molecules of gold.

"You increase the power of your microscope. You examine just one molecule of this gold. Now you see more supposedly empty spaces, with smaller whirling entities which you choose to call atoms.

"You examine one atom. The same result and you call the still smaller particles electrons. Down and down — who can say how far? Until, at last, you are looking into one intime. You see yet smaller particles whirling in space. That is the space between our stars!

"And these whirling points of light — perhaps you can distinguish no more than a million of them. They are the million largest, brightest of our stars. You cannot see our own sun; it is too small. Or our Earth — too small. And too dark.

"But if you did see our Earth, and were a fatuous scientist, you might say, 'Ah, at last I have seen the *smallest thing!*' Which is amusing, because our Earth has a good many rocks composing it. And each rock has a good many rocks composing it. And each rock goes down to pebbles, grains of sand, molecules, atoms, electrons — to infinity.

"Do you get the conception now? This whole universe we see and feel from here on Earth, from a greater viewpoint would all shrink into a tiny, apparently solid particle."

"I can visualize it," I said. "It's stupendous."

But Jim interposed, "This trip we are to make —"

Alice interrupted him, explaining, "Grandfather has been making tests. We have several models; he saved one of them to show you. We can see it now?" She looked inquiringly at her grandfather.

Dr. Weatherby rose to his feet. "We'll try it now. I'll show you the model and we'll send it . . . away.

"Come," he added. "When you see it start, you will under-stand."

We left the house. Night had closed down, a soft, cloudless night. Never had I seen the stars so brilliant.

Dr. Weatherby led us up a path, beneath spreading trees, past gardens of flowers, past his lake with its pool and a cas-cading brook for its outlet down the hillside to the Hudson; past the shadowy landing stage where high overhead my plane lay moored; up the slope of a hill to a long, narrow outbuilding.

Jim and I had noticed this building when we landed at dawn. It was new to us, erected during the year or so since we had last been here.

"My workshop," Dr. Weatherby said as we approached it.

I GAZED AT IT curiously. It was a single-story building, with-out windows, flat-roofed and no more than twenty feet high. In width, possibly thirty feet, but it was at least five times that long.

It lay crosswise on the hill. At a glance I could not guess of what materials it might be constructed. Wood, stone, metal — it seemed none of these. Its aspect was whitish, not silvery, or milky; rather was it a dead flesh white, with a faintly lurid cast of green to it.

In the starlight it lay silent and unlighted. But there seemed to it a glow, as though it were bathed in moonlight. And then I saw that the glow was inherent in it, almost a phosphorescence. Abruptly I felt that there was something uncanny, unnatural about this structure.

I made no comment. But I saw surprise on Jim's face, and at the lower end of the building where there appeared to be a door, he stopped, irresolute.

"Is . . . is the projectile in here?"

"Yes," said Alice. "Inside. But we're going to the test room first, aren't we, Grandfather?"

We went through a door and along a narrow passage. It was dimly illuminated by small blue vacuum tubes overhead. I found myself with Dolores.

"It's very wonderful," she said. "You will see, very soon. Oh, yes, where is Jim? I want Jim to see it."

"You're not afraid, Dolores? Afraid of the voyage they talk about?"

"Afraid? Oh, no!"

The passageway widened. "Here is Jim," I said. "Jim, stay with Dolores. She wants to show you this . . . this thing we've come to see."

We entered a room some thirty feet square. Dr. Weatherby switched on the lights. There were furniture, rugs, small tables of apparatus, instruments, and banks of vacuum tubes on tripods standing about, with wires in insulated cables connecting them. The cables littered the floor, like huge snakes.

Dr. Weatherby drew aside a portiere which cut off a corner of the room. Lying on a large table, flooded with a vacuum light from above, was a model of this building we were in. It was about two feet wide, by ten feet long — the same dead white, uncanny-looking structure.

A thought sprang to my mind. Was this building we were in itself the projectile? I think I murmured the question, for Dr. Weatherby smiled.

"No. Here is a small replica of the vehicle."

He unbolted the roof of the model. Resting inside was a tiny, dead white object about six inches long, cigarro-shaped, but with a pointed end and blunt stern. It rather suggested the ancient sub-sea vessels.

It had fin-shaped projections, like very small wings for its slow transit through air. A tiny tower was forward, on top, and there were bull's-eye windows lining the sides and in every face of the octagon tower.

Dr. Weatherby pointed out all these details to us, speaking in his low, earnest voice. "I'm wondering, Leonard, and you, Jim, if you are familiar with Elton's principle of the neutralization of gravity?"

"No," I said, and Jim shook his head. "Not in detail."

In 1988 Elton perfected it. I knew of it only as an electronic stream of radiant matter which when directed against a solid substance, destroyed — or partially destroyed — the attraction of that other substance for the Earth.

"I'll explain it when we get into the vehicle itself," Dr. Weatherby said.

He was connecting wires to the little model building on the table; and he closed its roof, and opened a wide doorway at its end. "I am going to charge this small building with the Elton current. The electronic stream will carry that tiny projectile with it.

"This will be the same as the start of our own voyage, Leonard, except that with this model, I have intensified the rapidity of the successive changes. What happens here in minutes, will take us hours. Sit down over there, all of you."

WE RANGED OURSELVES in the gloom across the room. The model of the building, and its end doorway open like an airplane hangar, was pointing past us. Jim and I sat together, with Alice near me, and Dolores by Jim. He put his arm around her.

A moment, and then Dr. Weatherby touched a switch. The room was plunged into darkness. From the table came a low electrical hum.

I strained my eyes. A glow was over there. It brightened. The little building on the table was glowing with a faint, blue-white light. A minute passed, or it might have been ten minutes. I do not know.

The hum of the Elton current intensified; a whir, then a faint, very tiny screaming throb. The building was now outlined completely; a luminous white, shot through with a cast of green, and red and yellow sparks snapping about it. From where I sat I could see partially into its open doorway, as the interior was not dark. It was glowing inside, and now I became aware of a very faint red stream, like light, pouring from the doorway, crossing the room, spreading like a fan.

It was the Elton ray, escaping its bonds, its tiny particles plunging outward with the speed of light, or more. The red glow stuck the blank, dead white wall of our room, stained the wall with its red sheen. Sparks were snapping in the air around me. To my nostrils came a faint, sulphurous smell. My skin was prickling.

"Look," whispered Alice.

The opposite wall where the red ray was striking, now seemed glowing of itself, a blank, opaque wall, stained red by the billions of imponderable particles bombarding it.

But it was no longer an opaque wall. Of itself it was now glowing, becoming translucent, transparent! The stars! Through the wall I could see the placid night outside, the dark hillside, the stars!

I felt Alice's hand gripping my arm. From the glowing model on the table, the tiny vehicle was issuing. The dead white thing. It came very slowly, floating out the doorway, as though drawn by the red diverging stream of light.

Slowly, it passed me, ascending a trifle, no longer dead white, for it was transfigured — alive now, shimmering, its outlines wavy, unreal. It moved a trifle faster, came to the wall of the room, passed through it.

"Watch," breathed Alice.

The vehicle — that tiny oblong shape smaller than my hand — was outside over the treetops, plunging onward in the red stream of light. Yet at that distance I could see it plainly, its image as large as when it was a few feet from my face.

And suddenly I realized I was staring after a thing gigantic. It showed now far over the hilltop. I could have sworn it was but some great air liner. A patch of stars was blotted out behind it.

Another moment; the silver thing off there was far away. Was it as far as the Moon? It was larger now than the Moon would have seemed, hanging out there!

I watched. I could still see it as plainly as when it started. But then suddenly came a change. Its image became fainter, thinner, and rapidly expanding. There was a faint image of it out there in the heavens, an image larger than the hillside.

There was an instant when I fancied that the image had expanded over all the sky — a wraith, a dissipating ghost of the projectile. It was gone. The stars gleamed alone in the deep purple of the night.

A click sounded. The hum of the Elton ray died into silence. The luminous wall of the room sprang into opaque reality.

I sat up, blinking, shivering, to find Dr. Weatherby standing before me.

"That, Leonard, is the start. Shall we see the vehicle itself?"

III

LAUNCHED INTO SPACE!

WE WERE TO LEAVE at dawn, and during the night a thousand details demanded out attention: Jim's resignation from the service, which he gave to the superior through verbal traffic department without so much as a word of explanation; my own resignation, leaving the post of Commander 3 of the 40 N temporarily to Argyle.

Temporarily! With what optimism I voiced it! But there was a queer pang within me; an exaltation — which I think was as well a form of madness — was upon us all. This thing we were about to do transcended all our petty human affairs.

I was standing at the door of the workshop, gazing at a tree. Its leaves were waving in a gentle night breeze, which as I stood there fanned my hot, flushed cheeks with a grateful coolness. I found Alice beside me.

"I'm looking at that tree," I said. "Really, you know I'll be sorry to leave it. These trees, these hills, the river — I wouldn't like to leave our Earth and never come back, Alice. Would you?"

"No," she said. Her hand pressed mine; her solemn blue eyes regarded me. She was about to add something else, but she checked herself. A flush rose to her cheeks; it mantled the whole column of her throat with red.

"Alice?"

"No," she repeated. "We'll come back, Len."

Dr. Weatherby called us. And Jim shouted, "This infernal checking! Len, come here and do your share. We're going at dawn. Don't you know that?"

I shall not forget the first sight I had of the vehicle. It lay in the great main room of the workshop. A hundred feet long, round like a huge cigarro, a dead white thing, lying there in the glow of the blue tubes.

Even in its silent immobility, there seemed about it a latent power, as though it were not dead, but asleep — a sleeping giant, resting quiescent, conscious of its own strength.

And there was about it too, an aspect almost infernal in its sleek, bulging body, dead-white like bloodless flesh, in its windows, staring like bulging, thick-lensed eyes. I felt instinctively a repulsion, a desire to avoid it. I touched it finally; its smooth side was hard and abnormally cold. A shudder ran over me.

But after a time these feelings passed. I was absorbed in examining this thing which was to house us, to bear us upward and away.

Within the vehicle was a narrow corridor down one side. Corridor windows opened to the left. To the right were rooms. Each had a window opening to the side, a window in the floor beneath, and in the roof above.

There was a room for Jim and me, another for Dolores and Alice, and one for Dr. Weatherby. An instrument and chart room forward, with a tower room for keeping a lookout, and a galley with a new Maxton electronic stove, fully equipped. And other rooms — a food room, and one crowded with a variety of apparatus: air purifiers, Maxton heaters and refrigerators, piping the heat and cold throughout the vehicle. There was a score of devices with which I was familiar, and another score which were totally strange.

Dr. Weatherby already had the vehicle fully equipped and provisioned. With a tabulated list of its contents, he and Jim were laboriously checking the items to verify that nothing had been overlooked.

"I don't want to know how it works," Jim had said. "Not 'til after we start. Let's get going. That's the main idea."

Then Alice took the list. She and Jim went from room to room. Dolores stood a moment in the corridor, as Dr. Weatherby and I started for the instrument room.

"Jim! Oh Jim, where are you?"

"He and Alice are farther back, Dolores." I said. "In the galley, I think. Don't you want to come forward with us?"

"I guess not. I'll go with Jim."

She joined them and I heard her say, "Oh, I'm glad to find you, Jim. I was a little frightened, just for a moment. I thought something was wrong here on board."

I turned and followed Dr. Weatherby to the instrument room.

WE STOOD before an instrument board of dials and indicators, with wires running upward to a score of gleaming cylindrical tanks overhead. A table was beside us, with a switchboard less complicated in appearance than I have seen in the navigating cages of many small liners.

There were chairs, a narrow leather couch across the room, and another table littered with charts and star-maps. And above it was a shelf, with one of the Grantline comptometers, the mathematical sensation of some years back. It was almost a human mathematical brain.

Under its keys the most intricate problem of calculus was automatically resolved, as surely as an ancient adding machine did simple arithmetic.

Dr. Weatherby began to show me the workings of the vehicle. "I need only give you the fundamentals, Leonard. Mechanically my apparatus here is fairly complicated. But those mere mechanics are not important or interesting. I could not teach you now, in so short a time, how to rectify anything which went mechanically wrong. I shall do the navigating.

"Indeed, as you will see presently, there is very little navigating involved. Mostly at the start — we must only be sure we collide with nothing and disturb nothing. When once we are beyond these planets, these crowding stars, there will be little to do."

I shook my head. "The whole thing is incomprehensible, Dr. Weatherby. That flight of your little model was almost gruesome."

"Sit down, Leonard. I don't want it to be gruesome. Strange, yes; there is nothing stranger, God knows, than this into which, frankly, I stumbled during my researches. I'll try to make the fundamentals clear. It will lose its uncanny aspect then. You will find it all as coldly scientifically precise as your navigation of the Fortieth North parallel."

He lighted my cigarro. "This journey we are about to make," he resumed, "involves but two factors. The first is the Eltonian principle of the neutralization of gravity. Sir Isaac Newton gave us fairly accurate formulae for the computation of the force of gravity. Einstein revised them slightly, and attempted to give an entirely different conception of celestial mechanics.

"But no one — except by a rather vague theory of Einstein's — has ever told us what gravity really is. What is this force — what causes this force — which makes every material body in the universe attract every other body directly in proportion to the mass and inversely as the square of the distance between them?

"Leonard, I think I can make it clear to you. There is passing between every material body, one with another, a constant stream of minute particles. A vortex of rotating particles loses some on one side, which fly off at a tangent, so to speak, and perhaps gains some upon the other side.

"Seventy-five years ago — about the time I was born, Leonard — they were talking of 'electrons', 'radiant energy', 'positive and negative disembodied electricity.' All different names for the same thing. The same phenomenon.

"All substance is of a very transitory reality. Everything is in a constant state of change. A substance builds up, or it breaks down. Or both simultaneously; or sometimes one and then the other."

"Electricity —" I began.

"Electricity," he interrupted, "as they used to know it, is in reality nothing but a concentrated stream of particles — electrons, intimes, call them what you will — moving from one substance to join another. Lightning is the same thing. Such a stream of particles, Leonard, is a tangible manifestation of gravitational force. They had it right before them, unrecognized. They called it 'magnetic force,' which meant nothing.

"How do these streams create an attractive force? Conceive the Earth and the Moon. Between them flow myriad streams of infinitesimal particles. Each particle in itself is a vortex — a whirlpool. The tendency of each vortex is to combine with the one nearest to it.

"They do combine, collide, whirl together and split apart. The whole, as a continuous, violently agitated stream, produces a continuous tendency toward combination over all the distance from the Earth to the Moon. The result — can't you see — must be a *force*, an inherent tendency pulling the Earth and the Moon together.

"Enough of such abstract theory! A while ago, I charged that little model of this building with an Elton ray. The model, and this building itself, are built of an ore of electrite, the one hundredth and fortieth element, as they called it when it was isolated a few years ago.

"You saw the model of the building glow? Electrons and intimes were whirling around it. The force communicated to the tiny projectile lying inside. In popular language, 'its gravity was destroyed.' Technically it was made to hold within itself inherent gravitation and the gravitation of everything else was cut off. It was, in the modern sense, magnetized, in an abnormal condition of matter."

I said, "There was a red ray from the little building. The projectile seemed to follow it."

"Exactly," he exclaimed. "That was the Elton Beta ray. It is flung straight out, whereas the Alpha ray is circular. The Beta is a stream of particles moving at over four hundred thousand miles a second. More than twice the speed of light!"

He chuckled. "When they discovered that, Leonard, the Einstein theories held good no longer. The ray bombarded and passed through the electric wall of the room, and the projectile went with it, drawn by it, sucked along by the inherent force of the flying whirlpools. The projectile with its infinitely greater mass than the mass of the flying particles of the ray, picked up speed slowly. But its density was lessening.

"As it gained velocity, it lost density. Everything does that, Leonard. I intensified the rapidity of the changes, as I told you. We shall take it slower. Hours, for what you saw in minutes."

He tossed away his cigarro and stood up over the instrument table. "When we start, Leonard, here is exactly what will happen. Our gravity will be cut off. Not wholly, I have only gone to extremes in describing the theory.

"With a lessened attraction from the Earth, the Moon will draw us. And passing it, some other planet will draw us onward. And later, the stars themselves."

He indicated his switches. "I can make the bow or the stern, or one side or the other, attractive or repulsive to whatever body may be nearest. And thus, in a measure, navigate. But that, Leonard, will be necessary for a few hours only, until we are well out beyond the stars."

He said it quite quietly. But I gasped. "Beyond the stars . . . in a few hours?"

"Yes," he said. "In our case, differing from my experiment with the model, we carry the Elton Beta ray, the 'red ray,' with us. The gravity principle we use only at the start, to avoid a possible collision. With the red ray preceding us, we will follow it. Ultimately at four hundred thousand miles a second.

"But the source of the ray, *being with us*, will give the ray constant acceleration, which we in turn will attain. Thus an endless chain of acceleration, you see? And by this I hope to reach the high speed necessary. We are going very far, Leonard."

"That model," I said, "grew larger. It spread — or did I fancy it? — over all the sky."

He smiled again. "I have not much left to tell you, Leonard. But what there is — it is the simplest of all, yet the most astounding."

Jim's voice interrupted us. "We've finished, Dr. Weatherby. Everything is aboard. It's nearly dawn. How about starting?"

The dawn had not yet come when we started. Dr. Weatherby's workmen were none of them in evidence. He had sent them away a few days before. They did not know his purpose with this vehicle; it was thought among them that he was making some attempt to go to the Moon. It was not a startling adventure. It caused very little comment, for since Elton's discovery many such projects had been undertaken, though all had not been successful.

Dr. Weatherby's activities occasioned a few daily remarks from the National Broadcasters of News, but little else.

There was, however, one of Dr. Weatherby's assistants, to whom he trusted with all his secrets: a young fellow called Mascar, a wordless, grave individual, quiet, deferential of manner, but with a quick alertness that bespoke unusual efficiency.

He had been on guard in the workshop since the workmen left. When Jim and I arrived, Dr. Weatherby had sent Mascar home for his much needed sleep. But he was back again, now before dawn, ready to stand at the Elton switch and send us away.

Dr. Weatherby shook hands with him, as we all gathered by the huge bull's-eye lens which was swung back to give ingress to the vehicle.

"You know what you are to do, Mascar. When we are well outside, throw off the Elton switch. Lock up the workshop and the house and go home. Report to the International Bureau of News that if they care to, they can announce that Dr. Weatherby's vehicle has left the Earth. You understand? Tell them they can assume, if they wish, that it will land safely on the Moon."

"I will do that," said Mascar quietly. He shook hands with us all. And his fingers lightly touched Dolores's head. "Good-bye, Miss Dolores."

"Good-bye, Mascar. Good-bye. You've been very good to Grandfather. I thank you, Mascar. You wait at home. We will be back soon."

"Yes," he said. He turned away, and I could see he was striving to hide his emotion.

He swung on his heel, crossed the room, and stood quiet, with a firm hand upon the Elton switch.

Jim called impatiently, "Come on, everybody. Let's get away."

For one brief instant my gaze through the forward opened end of the building caught a brief vista of the peaceful Hudson countryside. Hills, and trees in the starlight, my own Earth — my home.

The huge convex door of the vehicle swung ponderously closed upon us.

"Come to the instrument room," said Dr. Weatherby.

We sat on the couch, huddled in a group. The bull's-eye windows, made to withstand any pressure, were nevertheless ground in such a way that vision through them was crystal clear. The one beside me showed the interior of the workshop with Mascar standing at the Elton switch.

He had already thrown it. I could not hear the hum. But I saw the current's effect upon Mascar. He was standing rigid, tense, and gripping the switch as though clinging. And then, with his other hand, he seized a discharging wire planted near at hand, so that the current left him comparatively unaffected.

Still I could fee nothing. My mind was whirling. What was it I expected to feel? I do not know. Dr. Weatherby had assured us we would undergo no terrifying experience; he seemed to have no fear for the girls. But how could he be sure?

The walls of the workshop now were luminous; Mascar's motionless figure was a black blob of shadow in the glowing, snapping interior of the room. Sparks were crackling our there.

But here in the vehicle there was nothing save a heavy silence; and the air was cold, dank, tomblike.

THEN I FELT the current; a tingling; a tiny, infinitely rapid tingling of the vehicle. It was not a vibration; the electric floor beneath my feet was solidly motionless. A tingling seemed to pervade its every atom.

Then I realized my body was tingling! A whir, a tiny throbbing. It brought a sense of nausea and a giddiness. Involuntarily I stood up, trembling, reeling. But Dr. Weatherby sharply drew me back.

Alice and Dolores were clinging to each other. Jim muttered something incoherent. I met his smile, but it was a very weak, surprised, apprehensive smile.

I tried to relax. The nausea was passing. My head steadied. But the tingling grew more intense within me. It was a humming now. Not audible. A humming I could feel, as though every minute cell of my body was throbbing.

It was not unpleasant after a moment. A peculiar sense of lightness was upon me. A sense of freedom. It grew to an exaltation. I was being set free! Unfettered at last. But the mood upon me was more than an exaltation, an intoxication: a madness! I was conscious that Alice was laughing wildly.

I heard Dr. Weatherby's sharp command, "Don't do that! Look there; see the red ray?"

I clung to my reeling wits.

Jim muttered, "Look at it!"

The interior of the workshop was a whirling fog drenched in blood. I could see the red streaming out its open doorway.

"We're moving!" Alice cried. "Dolores, we've started!"

The enveloping room of the workshop seemed gliding backward. Not a tremor of the vehicle. Mascar's figure moved slowly backward and downward beyond my sight. The workshop walls were sliding past. The rectangle of its open end seemed expanding, coming toward us.

And then we were outside, in the starlit night. A dark hillside was dropping away. A silver ribbon of river was slipping beneath us, dropping downward, like a plummet falling.

The red ray had vanished. Dr. Weatherby's voice, calm now, with a touch of triumph to it that all had gone so well, said,

"Mascar has extinguished the red ray. We used it only for starting. We must start slowly, Leonard."

The river vanished. A huge Polar liner — I recognized its group of colored lights as Ellison's, flying in the forty thousand-foot lane — showed overhead. But it, too, seemed falling like a plummet. It flashed straight down past our window and disappeared.

Dr. Weatherby went to the instrument table. Time passed. It seemed only a moment or two though.

Dolores murmured, "Are we still moving, Jim? You must tell me. Tell me everything you see."

The room was stiflingly hot. We were all gasping.

"I've turned on the refrigeration," said Dr. Weatherby, "to counteract the heat of the friction of our passage through the atmosphere. It will be cool enough presently. Come over here. Don't you want to look down?"

We gathered over the instrument room's floor window. Stars were down there, white, red, and yellow stars in a field of dead black: a narrow crescent edge of stars, and all the rest was a gigantic dull red surface. Visibly convex! Patches of dark, formless areas of clouds. An ocean, the vaguely etched outlines of continents, the coastline of the Americas.

We were launched into space!

IV

EXPANSION!

THEN THE VEHICLE cooled rapidly. Soon we had the heaters going. The coldness of space enveloped us, penetrating the vehicle's walls. But with the heaters we managed to be comfortable.

Dr. Weatherby sat at the instrument table. His chronometer showed 5 A.M. We had started at 4 A.M. On one of the distant dials the miles were registering in units of a thousand. The dial-pointer was nearing XX6. Six thousand miles.

Dr. Weatherby glanced up as I appeared. Alice and Dolores, and Jim with them, had gone astern to prepare a broth. We were all of us still feeling a bit shaky, though the sense of lightness had worn off.

Dr. Weatherby had a chart on the table. It showed our solar system. The sun was at its center, and the planetary orbits in concentric circles around it. The planets and our own moon and a few of the larger comets and asteroids were all shown, their positions given progressively for each hour beginning at our starting time.

"I'm heading this way, Leonard. Holding the general plane in which the planets lie." His finger traced a line from the Earth, past the Moon, past Mars. Jupiter and Saturn lay over to one side, and Neptune to the other. Uranus was far on the opposite side, beyond the sun.

Dr. Weatherby added, "The Moon is drawing us now. But I shall shortly turn a neutral side toward it, and Mars will draw us. We are more than a freely falling body. We are being pulled downward."

I sat beside him. "What is our velocity now?"

He gestured toward a dial, an ingenious affair. He had already explained its workings, the lessening rate of the Earth's gravitational pull shown by a hair-spring balance as a figure on the dial.

"Three thousand miles an hour, Leonard." But as I watched, the figure moved to 4; and then to 5, 6, and 7.

The Moon, nearly full, lay below us, ahead of us, white, glittering, cold, with the black firmament and the stars clustering about it. We were falling bow down. Overhead, about our blunt stern, the giant crescent Earth hung across the firmament. It was still dull red; its configurations of land and water were plainly visible. A silver sunlight edged it.

"Ah, the sun, Leonard!" Abruptly we had emerged from the Earth's conical shadow into the sunlight. But the heavens remained black. The stars blazed with a cold, white gleam as before. And behind us was the white sun and its corona of flame leaping from it.

I HAVE SAID we were falling — our projectile falling bow down, like a plummet. Gazing through the window it seemed so. But the effect was psychological. I could as readily picture us on a level, proceeding onward.

It was as though we were poised within a giant hollow globe of black glass, star-incrusted. There could be no standards of up, or down; it was all as the mind chanced to conceive it. But within the vehicle itself, its soundless, vibrationless, level floor beneath our feet, a complete sense of normality remained.

"Dr. Weatherby," I said, "that model . . . you remember, it grew gigantic. But we . . . we're still the same size at which we started?"

For an hour past, a thousand questions had been seething in my mind. This navigation of space was clear enough. All my life scientists had been discussing it. We were moving now at a velocity of some twelve thousand miles an hour. But what was that? Less than the crawling of an ant using the equator of the Earth as a race track! Twelve thousand miles an hour — or twelve billion — would get us nowhere among the distant stars in a lifetime!

Dr. Weatherby answered my spoken question: "We are only very little larger than when we started, Leonard. An infinitesimal fraction, for our velocity is nothing as yet. I'll use the Elton Beta ray once we get farther out."

He turned to his switches. Through the window I saw the firmament swing slightly. He was navigating, heading for some distant realm beyond all the stars that we could see, all the stars that could exist out there. The tiny vehicle, threading its way. How did he, how could he possibly know his way?

I asked him bluntly, and he looked up from his chart with a smile. "Leonard, in five minutes I could tell you every remaining fundamental of the laws which are governing us. I will tell you, but I want Jim to hear it too. And I'm absorbed now in getting out past the asteroids. A little later, I'll make it clear."

We dropped past the Moon at a distance of perhaps a hundred thousand miles. We were then some two hundred and forty thousand miles from Earth. It was nearly noon, with the Earth standard time of Dr. Weatherby's home. We had been traveling eight hours; constantly accelerating, our velocity at noon had reached a thousand miles a minute.

The Moon, as we passed it, floated upward with a quite visible movement. It was a magnificent sight, though the smallest of telescopes on Earth brought it visually nearer than it was now.

We ate our first meal, slept, settled down to the routine of life on the vehicle. Another twelve hours passed. Our velocity had reached then a thousand miles a second. But that was only the one hundred and eighty-sixth part of the velocity of light!

We were now — with an average rate of five hundred miles a second from the time we left — some twenty-one million and six hundred thousand miles from Earth. Half way to Mars! But in four hours more the red planet floated upward past us. Dr. Weatherby kept well away — a million miles his instrument showed as he measured the planet's visible diameter.

We had now reached a velocity of some twenty thousand miles a second.

"I shall hold it at that," Dr. Weatherby said. "It's too crowded in here, too dangerous."

We transversed the asteroid region at about that rate. It was a tedious, tense voyage, so dangerous that for nearly five hours one of us was always at the tower window, to avoid a possible collision. The belt in her between the orbits of Mars and Jupiter was thick-strewn with asteroids. But none came near enough to endanger us.

We crossed Jupiter's orbit. Again Dr. Weatherby accelerated to one hundred thousand miles a second, but it was over an hour before we crossed Saturn's orbit, four hundred million miles further on. We went no faster for a time.

At this velocity it was tedious. Uranus's orbit at seventeen hundred million miles from the sun; Neptune at twenty-seven hundred million. And then that last outpost of the solar system, Xavion, discovered in 1964. The planet was at the opposite point of its orbit. We could not see it. Our own sun had long since dwindled into invisibility.

At last we were away! Launched into the realms of outer stellar space, plunging onward at a hundred thousand miles a second. But ahead of us the giant stars showed no change. As imperturbably distant in their aspect as when we started.

We, Jim and I, had had many hours of futile discussion: some in our own room, but more in the little tower where we sat on watch, gazing ahead at the motionless stars, our eyes at the small search-telescopes with which we swept the space into which the projectile was dropping.

We had seen many asteroids, but none near enough to be dangerous. And we passed the hours wondering what it was Dr. Weatherby had to tell us. How did he know where he was going? What was his direction? In all this chaos of immeasurable, unfathomable distance, of what avail to attempt any set direction? By what points could he navigate? It was unthinkable.

And more unthinkable: we had attained a maximum velocity of over one hundred thousand miles a second, only a little more than half the velocity of light. The *nearest* star we knew to be over four thousand light-years away. Light, traveling one hundred and eighty-six thousand, four hundred miles a second, took 4.35 years to reach that star. At this rate, we would take some eight years!

And this was the *nearest star!* Others were a thousand . . . tens of thousands . . . a hundred thousand times farther! Eighty thousand years, even eight hundred thousand years, we would have to travel to reach the distant nebulae! And even then, what realms of dark and empty space might lie beyond! It was unthinkable.

"He'll explain when he gets ready," said Jim.

AND HE DID. He called us into the instrument room, shortly after we crossed the orbit of Xavion. He spoke with a slow, precise phrasing: the careful phrasing of a scientist intent upon conveying his exact meaning.

"I think I told you once, Leonard, as a matter of actuality I stumbled upon this thing — these laws which are to govern our flight from now onward. They are definite laws, inherent in all matter.

"We are about to undergo an experience stranger, I think, than any man has undergone before. But not because of any intricate devices with which I have equipped this vehicle. Not at all. Merely the progressive workings of natural laws.

"I have experimented with them for some years. I think I understand them, though I am not sure. But their character, the actual, tangible result of what shortly will happen to us, that, I understand perfectly."

"What are the laws?" Jim demanded.

He gestured. "In a moment, Jim. I will say first that all this is merely a question of velocity. Matter, as it exists everywhere, is, as you well know, if varying states of velocity.

"And as the velocity changes, so does every other attribute of the substance. A group of electrons inherent in a lightning bolt, the intimes of a flying beam of light, are very different in temporary character from those of a bar of iron. But only different by virtue of their temporary velocity.

"Do I make myself plain? Any substance, for a very brief period, tends to maintain its integrity, its independent existence. But countless forces and conditions are assailing it. Wood burns, or rots. Iron rusts. The human body — a conglomeration of cells loosely clinging into a semblance of an independent entity — grows old, dies, disintegrates.

"Nothing is in a permanent state, a permanent condition of substance. The change may be slowly progressive. Or it may be sudden and violent.

"I'll be more specific. The Elton ray, acting upon the sensitive intimes of electrite, brings a sudden — and to that extent, unnatural — change.

"An added velocity was imparted to this vehicle and we left the Earth. The Elton current is operating the vehicle now. We have reached, or very nearly reached, the limit of velocity we can attain by using the force of celestial gravity — one hundred thousand miles a second.

"As I told you, however, we can now use the Elton Beta ray.

Our vehicle carrying the source of the ray forward, will presently attain a velocity —" He stopped, smiled gently, and added. "To our finite minds, it will be infinite. There will presently be no standards by which we can conceive it."

I would have interrupted him with a question, but he raised his hand. "In a moment, Leonard; then I want you and Jim to ask me any question you like. All this that I have said, is prefatory. The question is one solely of velocity. The rest is automatic. The natural laws governing the attributes of matter in relation to its velocity are these:

"First: A substance whose velocity is increased loses density proportionately. For instance, our vehicle, I consider it as a whole, you understand. As its velocity increases, it becomes less dense in substance. Comparatively less dense. Everything is comparative, of course. We ourselves have undergone the same change."

"A loss of density!" I exclaimed. "Then, of course, expanding, becoming more diffuse."

"Exactly, Leonard. And that is the second law. Our *size* is growing directly in proportion to our growing velocity."

I grasped it now. An infinite velocity had suddenly been imparted to the model of the vehicle. It had expanded, like a puff of vapor, over all the sky! Dr. Weatherby went on in his same careful voice.

"These two changes — a loss of density and a gain in size — have been going on ever since we left the Earth. They amount to little as yet. But presently I am going to increase our velocity immeasurably. External objects — the stars out there, you will see the change when you look at them.

"Do you understand me? The principle is obvious. A cold, dark star is small and dense. And moves slowly. A giant star is hot, of little density, and it has an enormous velocity." He paused.

Jim interjected, "I think we understand you, Dr. Weatherby. With this infinite velocity, we will pass beyond the stars. And growing in size . . . to be gigantic."

"So that, proportionately, the stars will shrink to atoms," said Alice.

Jim nodded. "Yes. I understand that. It sort of makes you gasp."

"But," I exclaimed, "Dr. Weatherby, you have held communication with other living minds, other beings, somewhere out here. Dolores's thought-waves."

"Yes," he said. "Thought-waves are infinitely faster than light. No one has ever —"

"I mean," I went on, "we are hoping to reach those other beings. But how — that is what Jim and I can't understand — how do you know where you are going? Might we not be heading directly away? Or perhaps Dolores is receiving the thought-waves progressively stronger and thus guiding us."

"No," Dolores spoke up. "It is difficult to receive the thoughts. There has been no time since we left —" She stopped, and added, "That makes me realize, didn't Alice leave us a moment ago?"

"Yes," said Jim. "It's time for lunch."

Dolores left her grandfather's side. "I must go help her."

Alice had slipped away quietly. Dolores now joined her in the galley.

Dr. Weatherby went on: "I remember remarking to you, Leonard, that there would be no need for navigation. We will grow, with an infinite velocity, to an infinitely gigantic size. Conversely, all this —" He waved his hand at the window, the firmament of white blazing suns — "all this immeasurable space we see out there will shrink to a size infinitely small. It will, later on, be smaller than our vehicle itself. Smaller than my body, my hand."

His voice rose to a sudden vehemence. "Don't you get the conception now? All this, our celestial space, will shrink to a pinhead — an atom. We will emerge from it into some tremendous greater emptiness, some greater space. As much greater as the space of a bedroom interior would be to the head of a pin lying on a bureau! What matter whether we emerge on one side of the pinhead or the other? The distance will be infinitesimal!"

What matter indeed! I clung to the conception. So simple, yet so vast! And suddenly there sprang before me a vision of our little Earth back there, already invisible, circling its tiny orbit, a mere nothing in the cosmos of infinite nature. An electron! Less than that—the merest infinite particle of an electron.

This whole universe of stars, merely a cluster of tiny particles, clinging together to form an atom of something else! And trillions of such atoms making up the head of a pin, lying on someone's bureau!

Dr. Weatherby's voice quieted. "Suppose ultimately, we were to cross our atom and emerge in exactly the wrong direction. We would find no vastly great emptiness, but merely other atoms like our own, going downward, so to speak, into the pin's head, instead of merging from it.

"But that cannot happen. Nature, in all its natural phenomena, always chooses the path of least resistance. We could not increase our velocity without adequate distance to transverse, nor increase our size without adequate emptiness to fill.

"You see! We may be going wrongly now. It makes no difference; the ultimate distance will be infinitesimal. But I know that by all natural laws we are seeking greater spaces. We will find, beyond these stars, an infinitely greater emptiness.

"Our size ultimately will fill it. But we will have turned to seek an emptiness still vaster, until, at last, freed from these clusters of substance which themselves are clinging together to form that pinhead, we will emerge."

V

EMERGING FROM INFINITE SMALLNESS

ALICE AND I WERE sitting in the small round tower that projected some six feet above the top of the vehicle, near its forward end. Through the windows here — eight of them, and one above us — the huge, inverted black bowl of the heavens lay fully exposed.

Myriad swarms of stars were thick-strewn everywhere. Freed from the distortion of the Earth's atmosphere, they blazed like balls of molten fire: white, blue-white, yellow and red. Red giants and dwarfs, the old and the young, occasionally a comet with its million miles of crescent, fan-shaped tail.

Clusters of stars appeared, blended by distance; binaries, revolving one upon the other; multiple stars; single white-hot suns blazing victorious with their maturity. And far off the spiral nebulae — patches of stardust, suns being born anew, or complete, separate universes. It was a glorious, awesome sight!

The red Elton Beta ray now preceded us. From here in the tower we could see it, flashing ahead like a dim searchlight beam. We had picked up velocity rapidly, had reached now some three hundred and sixty thousand miles a second, nearly twice the speed of light. Yet in all this scene, these whirling stars at which we were plunging, there was no visible movement. To an ant, crawling along a hillside ledge, the distant mountains seemed coming no nearer.

The dials showed our velocity to have reached very nearly one light-year per hour. No longer was it possible to use the unit of miles; our instruments showed now only light-years. Light travels 186,400 miles a second, and in our Earthly year there are

31,536,000 seconds. A light-year, then — the distance light can speed in a year — represents 5,883,000,000,000 miles. This sum now was our smallest unit of measurement.

We were now 4.25 light-years from Earth. Alpha Centauri, nearest of all the stars to Earth at 4.35 light-years, loomed ahead of us. I stood at one of the forward windows regarding it. Two stars it is, in reality, for it is a binary.

Its components were beginning visually to separate now: two white blazing suns, millions of miles apart, slowly revolving upon a common center with a revolution that took thousands of years.

Yet, as I stood there, I fancied I could see them turning! We were heading directly for them; they were leaping up out of the void. There was a slow but visible movement throughout the firmament now. The stars in advance of us were opening up, spreading apart, drifting past our side windows, closing together again behind us. Dr. Weatherby was at my elbow.

"I shall keep away from Centauri," he remarked. "And presently, we must go faster, Leonard."

He went to his instrument table. The red Beta ray preceding us seemed to intensify a trifle; the firmament shifted slightly as our direction was altered. As I stood there, in ten minutes or so, the twin blazing suns of Alpha Centauri came up and swept past us.

I hastened to a side window to watch them. Blazing giants they were, floating off there a million miles away, each of them so large that our huge sun would have been a match flame beside them.

But suddenly I wondered, blinked, and stared with my breathing stopped by the shock of it. Were these indeed blazing giants a million miles off there? Or were they white points of fire a mile away? Abruptly my whole viewpoint changed. I saw these stars, all the blazing white points in the firmament, not as giant suns unfathomably distant, but only as small glowing eyes quite close.

These were gleaming eyes in a black night, gleaming eyes close around me. Eyes no larger than my own! Our vehicle . . . myself — gigantic! I realized it now. All this unfathomable distance around me had shrunk. I saw our giant vehicle floating very slowly, very sedately onward between the staring, crowding eyes.

Dr. Weatherby smiled when I told him. "It is all in the viewpoint, Leonard. In my computations I shall cling to the viewpoint of Earth. Miles then light-years. Earthly standards of time, distance, and velocity. But shortly we shall have to abandon them entirely. Sit down, Leonard. I want to talk to you. Where is Dolores?"

"In the galley, I think." I said, sitting down at the instrument table beside him.

"I don't want Dolores to hear me. I've been wondering whether I should try and have her communicate again with the outside. It has been a month since we did that."

This, almost more than any other aspect of our adventure, interested me. "Tell me about those thought communications, Dr. Weatherby."

"There is nothing else to tell. There seem to be two . . . shall we call them people? A young man and a girl. They are in dire distress. The man is intelligent — more so than we are, I should judge. He was surprised to have us answer him."

"Does he know where we are?"

"No, I think not. But when I told him, he seemed to understand. Dolores gets, not words, but ideas, which naturally she can only translate into our English words. But, Leonard, I do not conceive these beings will be physically of an aspect very different from ourselves. We are . . . so close to them."

"Close!"

He smiled. "Quite close, Leonard. One of them might be holding us — our whole universe — on the palm of his hands. An inch from a thumb, a foot from his ear. I was thinking of that when I was trying to fathom the possible velocity of thought-waves. It's all in the viewpoint. His thoughts would not have to travel far to reach us. His brain gives orders to his muscles in a fraction of a second over a far greater distance."

The dials showed us to be ten thousand light-years from Earth, our velocity fifty light-years an hour, when Dr. Weatherby called to us all to assemble in the instrument room. Days, or what would have been days on Earth, had passed since we started.

I had lost all count, though upon Dr. Weatherby's charts the relative time-values were recorded. We ate regularly, slept when we could.

Dr. Weatherby was tired, almost to the point of exhaustion,

for though Jim, Alice and I alternated on watch in the tower, Dr. Weatherby remained almost constantly at his instrument table.

Ten thousand light-years from Earth! But ahead of us the star-points stretched unending.

Dr. Weatherby faced us. "We are not going fast enough. I have not dared, but now I must. I want you all to understand. I have had the red Beta ray at very nearly its weakest intensity. I am going to turn it on full, to the intensity I used for the model.

"There will be a shock, but only momentarily. You, Leonard, go to the tower. If anything too large or too dense for safety seems coming at us, you can warn me."

He smiled. "But we will encounter nothing of the sort, I am sure. I'll sit here at the controls. The rest of you I suggest stay here with me for a while."

I went to the tower. Ahead of us was the faint stream of the red ray. The star-points were floating past us, opening to our advance, streaming past, overhead, to the sides, and beneath, and closing after us. Even with my greater viewpoint, the points of fire were passing swiftly now. Some were very near: they seemed like white sparks. I fancied I could have reached out and struck them aside with my hand.

Dr. Weatherby's voice reached me as I sat in the tower. "Ready!"

I seemed to feel, or to hear, a hum, a trembling. I saw the Beta ray flashing ahead of us with a deeper, more intense red, but for a moment it reeled before my gaze. The nausea I had had at starting from Earth recurred. I closed my eyes, but only momentarily, for the sickness passed as before.

Dr. Weatherby's voice called to me, "All right, Leonard?"

"Yes," I responded.

The scene outside my window was a chaos: flashing points of fire. How could we avoid them? Showers of white sparks rushing at us. I tried to shout a warning, but instead I laughed with a touch of madness. Avoid them! Millions of them were already colliding with us! Sparks showering impotently against our sleek electrite sides.

And then I realized that these sparks, these stars, were passing through us! A steady, flashing stream of them. I could see their luminous white points beaming within the vehicle as the stream flowed through.

Stars no longer. Why, these were mere imponderable electrons! Some were dark, shining only by reflected light — worlds like our earth. But I knew they were not imponderable bodies passing through the density of our vehicle. The reverse.

It was we who were the less dense. Our vehicle comparatively was a puff of vapor, through which these tiny bodies were passing.

A stream of electricity, myriad electrons flowing through a copper wire, are not less dense than the wire. The electrons are the densities; imponderable, of a mass imperceptible, because they are infinitely small. But of a tremendous density; it is the wire which is ponderous.

So now with us. I sat bewildered, for how long I cannot say. I heard at intervals Dr. Weatherby's voice: "Light-years a hundred thousand. One million. Ten. One hundred million."

We were a hundred million light-years from Earth! The flashing points of fire continued to stream past. But there was a change, a thinning in advance of us; a clustering white radiance behind.

I sat motionless, tense. It might have been minutes, or an hour.

I found Dr. Weatherby beside me, and I turned to him. I was stiff, cramped and cold. I tried to smile. "We're all right . . . still, Dr. Weatherby."

"Look," he said. "We're beyond them."

A darkness loomed ahead. To the sides the brilliant star-points seemed rushing together; clustering to form other, fewer white points. And the whole, sweeping backward into the seething radiance which lay behind us. Soon it was all back there, a shrinking white mist of fire; billions of seething particles of stardust shrinking together.

"Watch it, Leonard. It is our universe. Watch it go!"

We turned to the rear window. Everywhere now was empty blackness, except directly behind us. A silver mist hung back there in the void. It was dwindling. Then I saw it as a tiny, flattened, lens-shaped silver disk. But only for an instant, for it was shrinking fast.

A lens-shaped disk! A point of white light! A single faint star — a single entity. No . . . not a star; nothing but an electron!

For a breath I realized how near it was. A single tiny white spark, trembling outside our window. I could have pinched it with my thumb and finger.

It trembled, vanished into blackness.

A DAY PASSED, a day to us because we ate our meals, and slept. But to the worlds, the universes outside our windows, congealing behind us into single points, winking and vanishing into an oblivion of space and time, this day of ours was an eternity.

Our dials had long since become useless, a billion light-years from our starting point. A billion billion, and even that dwindling with our changing standards and viewpoint into a space we could have held in our cupped hands. Of what use to try and measure it. Or even conceive it.

The black, empty firmament had only remained empty for a moment. Ahead and off to the sides other luminous points showed. For hours Dr. Weatherby and I sat together watching them.

There was a moment when a single star gleamed far ahead. But soon it was a spiral of whirling stardust. It spread to the sides as we leapt at it. And every myriad particle of it suddenly showed as a tiny swirling mist of yet other particles.

They spread gigantic, each of them a nebula — a universe. One of them whirled directly through us, a white stream of tumbling radiant dust. Behind us it shrank again to a single point. And the billion other points shrank into one. And the one faded and was gone.

A night of this. Was our own universe an electron? I realized it could hardly have been that. Call it an intime. If we had encountered it now, it would have been too small for our sight. The tiniest swirling particle flashing through us now was composed of billions of universes as large as our own.

The night passed. We sat calmly eating our morning meal. The human mind adjusts itself so readily! Physical hunger is more tangible than the cosmos of the stars. Dr. Weatherby gestured toward the windows where the points of luminous mist momentarily were very remote.

"I should say that we . . . this vehicle is larger than any intime now. Possibly larger than electrons.

"Soon we will find ourselves among the atoms, and the molecules. There will then be a change. Very radical.

"A little more coffee, Alice, please. Presently I am going to try and erect our electro-telescope. Then I must get a little sleep."

He seemed, indeed, upon the verge of exhaustion.

THERE WAS A slow change all that day. These glowing things we were passing — universes, stars, or electrons or intimes, call them what you will — they seemed now more uniform; those at a distance, more like opaque globules, gray. And they seemed almost solid and cold. Yet it was the illusion of distance only, for we passed through several of them — streams of white fire mist as always before.

At noon, a black void of emptiness surrounded us. It was the longest, the most gigantic we had encountered, an hour of it.

Then again a point showed. It spread to the sides of us. But it was different. I could not say how. It was vague, gray. It streamed past, very distant on both sides and beneath us. At one moment I fancied it appeared as a distant, gigantic enveloping curtain, gray and vague. But then I thought it was a film of tiny globules, solid, entities, unradiant.

I called Dr. Weatherby. But before he arrived, the grayness had all slipped behind us. He saw it as a gray, formless blob. It congealed to a point. And then it vanished.

"That was an atom, Leonard," he said. His voice had an excitement in it. "That was our first sight of anything of the new realm large enough to have an identity. Substance, Leonard! The substance of which our universe, our Earth, is so infinitesimal a part. Everything we see now will be identical with it. The atoms! We are emerging!"

THEY AROUSED ME from sleep some hours later, calling me excitedly. I found them all in the instrument room crowded around Dolores, who was sitting on the couch, her hands pressed against her forehead. Jim cried; "She's getting thought-waves, Len! Someone is communicating with her!"

Dr. Weatherby was murmuring, "What is it, Dolores? Do you get it clearer now?"

"Yes. Someone is thinking: *We can see you! We see you coming!*"

"Yes, Dolores. What else?"

"That's all. *We're watching! We see you coming!*"

Jim murmured in a low voice, "The man on the cliff! The young man and the girl in distress!"

Dolores shook her head. "No. This is someone else. Closer. Stronger. The thoughts are very strong."

"Can't you see anything, Dolores?" Dr. Weatherby touched her, shook her gently. "Try, child. Tell them to think about themselves."

"I see —" she stopped, then stammered; "I see . . . a light. A very big light. There are people —"

"Men?"

"Yes. Men. Three or four of them. Sitting near a light. It shines so white. It hurts." But she put her hand, not to her eyes but to her temple. "I'm thinking to them, *Why can't I see you? I want to see you!* Wait. Now, I understand. He, someone thinks at me, *Try your telescope! Haven't you a telescope? Soon you will see us. We have seen you for a very long time.*"

Alice blurted out, "How long, Dolores? Ask them that?"

"No," commanded Dr. Weatherby. "That's absurd. Dolores —"

But her hands had dropped from her forehead. "It's gone. I'm tired. My head is tired."

Jim drew me to the window. "Look there! I was on watch. When this began appearing I called everybody. But then suddenly Dolores began getting the thoughts."

THE SCENE OUTSIDE was wholly changed. Beneath us, to the sides and ahead, a grayness stretched, a continuous solid grayness. Elusive, formless, colorless; I could not guess how distant it might be save that it stretched beyond the limits of my vision. But ahead and above us, the scene was not gray. A vague, luminous quality tinged the blackness up there. Luminous, as though a vague light were reflected.

There was no visible movement anywhere. But presently, as one staring at a great motionless cloud will see its shape in changing, I began to see changes. The flat gray solidity was not flat, but hugely convex. And it was slowly turning. Huge convolutions of it were, slowly as a cloudbank, taking new forms. And all of it was slowly moving backward.

Then we came to the end of it. Black emptiness ahead. Behind us was a gray-massed, globular cloud. Then another, its twin fellow, came rolling up beneath us in front, spread to the sides, shrank again behind us.

"Molecules," said Dr. Weatherby. "See how they're dwindling!"

I saw presently, swarms of them, always smaller. And ahead

of us they seemed congealed into a gray solidity — a substance, it was passing beneath us, and to the sides.

Again quite unexpectedly, my viewpoint changed. I saw our vehicle plunging upward, its pointed bow held upward at an angle. A solidity was around us; to the sides, gray, smooth curtains; overhead a glow of white in a dead black void.

A black void? My heart leaped. That was not blackness up there above our heads! It was blue! Color! The first sight of color. A blue vista of distance, with light up there. Light and air!

Beside us the smooth gray walls were smooth no longer. Huge jagged rocks and boulders, a precipice! We seemed in some immense canyon, slowly floating upward. But it was a dwindling canyon. And then abruptly we emerged from it.

I saw its walls close together beneath us. An area of gray was down there; gray with a white light on it. The light made sharp inky shadows on a tumbling naked waste of rock.

The gray area was shrinking to a blob, a blob of gray shining in a brilliant light. Directly beneath us, stretching to the horizon on both sides, lay an undulating white level surface. The single blob of gray was down there on it. And off in the distance, where the surface seemed abruptly to end, gigantic blurs loomed into the blue sky.

Dr. Weatherby was calling me to the tower. I found him trembling with eagerness. "Leonard, I have the electro-telescope working. Look through it."

I gazed first through the front and overhead tower windows. The white disk filled a perceptible area of the sky. But it was not like a sun; it seemed rather a smooth, flat disk with light behind it, a white disk with a dark narrow rim. Clear, cloudless sky was everywhere else. And very far away, behind and above the white disk, I saw a gigantic, formless, colorless shape towering into the blue of distance.

"Look through the telescope, Leonard."

I gazed upward through the electro-telescope. Its condensing lens narrowed the whole gigantic scene into a small circular field of vision. I gasped. Wonderment, awe swept over me. The blue sky was the open space of a tremendously large room: I saw plainly its ceiling, floor and distant walls.

The giant shape was a man. He was bending forward over a table — the table was under me. The man's hunched shoulders and peering face were above me.

For an instant my mind failed to grasp it all. I swung the telescope field downward, sidewise, and up again. And then at last I understood. This was a room, with men grouped at this nearer end of it around a table — men of human form, intent faces framed with long, white hair.

The undulating surface over which our vehicle was floating was a slide of what seemed glass, a clear glass slide with a speck of gray rock laying in its center. And the white disk over us in the sky was the lower, small lens of a microscope through which these men were examining us!

VI

THE NEW REALM

TWENTY DAYS! So full of strange impressions I scarcely know how to recount them. Yet, after such a trip, they were days of almost normality.

Our vehicle beneath that microscope had grown rapidly in size. And with our expanding visual viewpoint, and the nearness of solid, motionless objects, its velocity seemed infinitely small. It barely floated past the microscope, settling to the floor of that huge room; and with a normal proportionate size, the Beta ray shut off, it came to rest.

They crowded around us — old men, loosely robed, and with flowing white hair, seamed, smooth, hairless faces, stern but kindly, and eyes very bright and intelligent.

They crowded around us, at first timid, then friendly, talking together excitedly in a strange, liquid tongue.

Dr. Weatherby tried to greet them and to shake hands. They understood neither his words, nor the gesture. But in a moment they comprehended. And shook hands, all of them with each of us, very solemnly.

The room had oval openings for windows; light was outside but it seemed rather dim. Presently one of the men tried to herd us along the wall of the room.

"No!" said Dr. Weatherby. "Don't go! We must stay in the vehicle!"

But when we turned toward it the men resisted us with a sudden stubborn force.

"Don't!" I shouted. "Jim, stop that! We'd better go with them."

The old men seemed to have gone into a sudden panic of violence.

They were pushing, shoving us. They obviously had little strength, but the commotion would draw others from outside.

We yielded, and they herded us down the long room. A panel slid aside. We crossed a long, narrow viaduct, a metallic bridge with high parapet sides. We seemed to be a hundred feet in the air.

I caught a vista of low-roofed buildings: verdure — giant flowers on the roof, streets down there, and off in the distance a line of hills.

The air was soft and pleasant. Overhead was a blue sky, with gay white masses of clouds. There seemed to be no sun. The light was stronger than twilight, but flat, shadowless.

At the opposite end of the viaduct the ground seemed rising like a hill. A small mound-shaped building was there: a house with a convex roof which had a leveled platform on one end, a platform banked with vivid flowers.

It seemed a two-storied building, built of smooth, dull-gray blocks. Balconies girdled it. There were windows, and a large, lower doorway, with a broad flight of circular stairs heading up the hill to it.

Our viaduct led us into the second floor of the house. We entered on a large room, an oval, two-story room so that we found ourselves up on a sort of second-story platform, midway from floor to ceiling.

Low couches were here, a row of them with sliding panels of what might have been paper dividing them. The platform, this second story, was some thirty feet, broadly oval. It had a low, encircling railing; a spiral staircase led downward to the main floor of the apartment.

I saw furniture down there of strange, unnatural design, a metallic floor splashed with vivid mosaic pattern, a large gray frame, ornately carved, with a great number of long strips stretched across it, strings of different length. It seemed not unlike an enormous harp lying horizontal.

Narrow windows, draped with dark gauze, were up near the ceiling. They admitted a dim light. This whole interior was dim, cool and silent. A peace, a restfulness pervaded it. And our captors — if captors they were — seemed more like proud hosts. They were all smiling.

But when they left a moment later, I fancied that they barred the door after them.

"Well," said Jim. "I can say that this is very nice. Let's look things over, and then go to bed. I'm tired out, I can tell you that. Say, Dolores, it just occurred to me — these fellows can't understand a word we say. But you were thinking thoughts to them a while ago, and you understood each other. Why don't you try that now?"

It had occurred to me also. Why had these people understood Dolores's thoughts, when her words were incomprehensible? Were thoughts, then, the universal language? Tiny vibrations which each human brain amplified, transformed into its own version of what we call words? It seemed so.

Dolores was clinging closely to Alice's hand. In these unfamiliar surroundings she was at a loss to move alone.

"I did," she answered Jim. "I tried . . . but there was so much noise. They could not hear me."

"Try now," said Dr. Weatherby.

"I will. I am." She stood motionless, hands to her forehead.

There was a long silence. Then she said, "I think . . . yes, someone thought to me, *The Man of Language will come to you.*"

"Is that all, Dolores?"

"Yes. That's all. It's gone."

"The Man of Language!" Jim exclaimed. "An interpreter! Dolores, what about that young man and girl who were in distress? They were out here, weren't they?"

"I don't know. I never get their thoughts now."

"Try."

"I have tried. They may get mine. I can't say. But they never answer."

They brought us food, meals at intervals, strange food which now I shall not attempt to describe. But we found it palatable; soon we grew to like it. Then a man came, whom afterward we learned to call the Man of Language. He wore a simple garment, a queerly flaring robe, beneath which his naked legs showed.

His face was smooth, hairless. But the hair on his head was luxuriant. His head, upon a stringy neck, was large, with a queer distended look, and with veins bulging upon his forehead.

Yet withal, he was not grotesque. A dignity sat upon him. His dark eyes were extraordinarily brilliant and restless. His smile of thin, pale lips was kindly, friendly. He shook hands with each of us. But he did not speak at first. He sat among us, with those restless eyes regarding, observing our every detail.

We soon found he knew no word of our language. He had come to learn it, to have us teach it to him. We were made aware, later, that all these people, compared to ourselves, had memories that were extraordinarily retentive. But this man, he called himself Ren, was even for them, exceptional. His vocation was to learn, and to remember.

He began with simple objects: eyes, nose, and mouth. Hands, a table, a bed. As though he were a child, we pointed out our eyes, and named them; one eye, two eyes, a finger, two, three, four fingers.

It seemed like a game. When we told him once, it was never forgotten. But it was a game which to us, even under such conditions, soon became irksome. We were impatient. There was so much we wanted to know. And though we never tried to leave this building in which we were housed, it was obvious we were virtual prisoners.

Ren came away every time of sleep. He stayed hours; his patience, his persistence were inexhaustible. We took turns with him, each of us for an hour of two at a time. Occasionally Dolores would try to make something clear by thinking it. It helped. But he did not like it. It was necessary for him virtually to go into a trance before he could receive Dolores' thoughts.

Gradually Ren was talking to us, broken sentences at first, then with a flow surprisingly voluble. He used queerly precise phrases, occasionally a sentence inverted; and with a strange accent of pronunciation indescribable.

We had tried to question him when first he could talk. But he avoided telling us anything we wanted to know, save that once, at Dr. Weatherby's insistence, he assured us that our vehicle was safe. And that the small fragment of rock beneath the microscope — that tiny gray speck which held our universe, our Earth — was guarded so that no harm could come to it.

This was a city, the capital, the head city of a nation. Its people had lived here on this globe since the dawn of their history, ascended from the beasts which even now roamed the air, the caves, forests, and the sea.

Ren smiled at us. "You too," he said. "I can realize you are of an origin the same."

He did indeed think we were of a human type very primitive. The men of science who had seen us coming out of infinite smallness beneath their microscope, had remarked on it.

The small protuberance in the corner of our eyes, the remains of the beasts' third eyelid, the shape of our heads, our almost pointed ears — I notice that his own were very nearly circular — our harsh voices, our thick, stocky, muscular bodies were indications that they remarked on.

We discussed it. But Jim interrupted. "How did your men of science know that we were coming out of that piece of gray rock?"

It had been partly by chance. The fragment of rock had been a portion of the interior wall of a room wherein scientific experiments were being made. Ren used our words, "Experiments in physics and chemistry."

One of the scientists had found himself receiving strange thought-waves. Ren described them. They were Dolores's thoughts. The scientist traced them with measuring instruments to the wall of the room, but could be no more exact than that.

Then, later, from a tiny protuberance of the wall, a glow was observed. It proved to be a sudden radio-activity; this protuberance of gray stone had become radiant. Electrons were streaming off from it. The scientists clipped it off the huge block of stone of which it was so small a part, and put it under the microscope. It was violently radioactive. And from it they observed a stream of red.

"Our Beta ray," Dr. Weatherby exclaimed. "Our voyage, the disturbance we set up made the substance give off its electrons."

"Yes," nodded Ren. "They think so. They examined it beneath the lens, and after a little while they saw you."

Alice said, "My sister was getting thoughts from here." She told him about the mysterious young man and girl, threatened by some unknown danger, a strange cliff, the young couple at bay upon a ledge, the valley beneath them filled with a nameless horror.

REN'S FACE CLOUDED. "Yes. We have had thoughts from them. But now the thoughts have stopped. Those two are the children of our ruler. You would call him our king? They are the young prince and his sister, the princess.

"A year ago they both disappeared. A year, that is ten times daylight and darkness. We did not know why they went, or where. Run away, or perhaps stolen from us, for our king is very old and of health quite bad. Soon the prince will be king.

"But they disappeared. There is a very . . . a horrible savage people in the forests beyond the great caves. You spoke it truly, my lady Alice. They are a nameless horror; we do not often speak of things like that. We fear our prince and princess may be there.

"And here at home there is a growing trouble as well. Our women, the young girls particularly, are very restless and aggrieved. They do not like their lot in life. Some already are in rebellion.

"On the great island is a colony of virgins, where no man may go. We thought . . . we hope that perhaps the virgins had stolen our prince and princess, to hold them as hostages that we may be forced to yield to the virgins' cause."

"The prince and princess stolen," Jim exclaimed, "and you have done nothing about it?"

Ren smiled gently. "We have done a great deal, but to no purpose has it been as yet. We got the prince's thoughts. He was asking us for help. But he would not say what threatened, and he could not say where he was, for he did not know. And then the thoughts suddenly stopped.

"Oh, yes, we have searched. The island of the virgins was invaded. But the virgins — indeed no woman of our nation — will admit knowing anything of our prince. We have organized an army. All the nearer forests have been searched. And now we are getting ready to invade the caves. But it is not easy to get men for our army. That nameless horror —"

His voice held an intonation almost gruesome. He changed the subject abruptly.

"Our king, very shortly now he will want to see you. He feels, perhaps, you can aid us. You men, of strength, and these two young women — they might perhaps be of assistance in dealing with our virgins. But you will have to be examined, your minds gauged, so we may know if your oath of allegiance is honorable."

"By the infernal, mine will be!" Jim exclaimed. "I'll go with your army to the caves, nameless horror, or not."

Jim, with Ren, later joined me. And then Dr. Weatherby approached. "Where are the girls?" he asked.

They were in another part of the building. I noticed Dr. Weatherby gazing downstairs with a furtive air, as though he had come here to join us, knowing the girls were not here, and not wanting them around.

Jim was saying, "You think, Ren, that tomorrow — I mean after our next sleep — that the king will want to see us?"

"Yes," answered Ren. "Perhaps tomorrow."

"When we've taken the oath," Jim added, "they'll let us out of here, won't they. If we're going to join your army."

Dr. Weatherby sat down among us. He said to Ren, "You spoke of your king being in ill-health. Do you have much sickness, much disease, here?"

"No," replied the old man. "Our climate is healthy. Our people have always been so. There is very little —"

"I mean . . . perhaps you have doctors, men of medicine, who are quite skillful?"

"Yes. There are such. In the past they have been very learned. The records of history —"

"And surgeons, perhaps, very skillful surgeons?" Dr. Weatherby was leaning forward; his hands, locked in his lap, were trembling.

Ren said abruptly, "What do you mean?"

"I mean . . . my granddaughter, Dolores, she is blind."

The man nodded gravely. "That is so. It is very sorrowful. I have seen others here. It is a terrible affliction."

"But your surgeons, Ren. I have dared hope that she might be cured."

There was a moment of breathless silence. A pity for Dr. Weatherby swept me. Ren would shake his head: he would say, "No, she cannot."

But he said, "Why, it could of course be done."

"There is the question of an eye available."

"You mean you wonder about a transfer. It is strange, but even though we are so different," Ren said, "our eyes are identical in structure."

Dr. Weatherby went into further details concerning the complications of Dolores's blindness, but Ren shrugged away its import. "It can be done," he repeated. "And there is a man who will give us the missing link. Loro, a criminal who must die. He is repentant now. At his trial he pleaded that he might live long enough to expiate his crimes.

"Loro will volunteer. I know it."

VII

THE SACRIFICE

"ARE YOU SURE she will see when they take the bandages off?"

"I think she will, Alice. They say she will."

"But we don't know. I wish she'd awaken. We can take the bandages off then, can't we?"

"Yes. Dr. Weatherby will do it."

Alice tiptoed across the room and back. "She's still asleep. I wish she'd awaken. Will it have to be as dim as this in here?"

"Yes, I think so. Dimmer, maybe. They're afraid of the first light for her."

The intricate, deeply involved operation had evidently created a widespread interest throughout the city. Surgeons had come, examined Dolores, held innumerable conferences, examined Loro, whose eyes, as they had suspected, could be used with perfect satisfaction. They anticipated there would be no difficulties. This was their decision after their final conference: they were capable of giving sight to Dolores.

We had not yet been out for our audience with the king. Nothing more had been said concerning it; the operation had become all-absorbing to everyone. The city quite obviously was in an excitement over it, an excitement only surpassed by our own publicly unexplained presence.

They had taken little Dolores up to our rooftop, where, from below, a curious throng gazed up at her. And then taken Loro. I heard the wild cheering.

I had wondered why they would not take one eye only, that each might see. But they had told me that it was impossible. In this instance, a lone one transplanted could not survive. There were technical, deeply medical reasons for this. I did not pry into these.

Then they brought Dolores back. Her eyes were bandaged.

Hours passed. The healing fluid they said was very swift. When Dolores awoke we could remove the bandages. Alice and I sat together.

Dr. Weatherby entered with Jim. Behind them, lingering near the doorway, was the chief surgeon who had performed the operation. He said softly, "You can awaken her. A little less light. Then you can take the bandages off."

We awakened her gently. She sat up weakly, in bewilderment. "Oh, the bandage, yes, I remember now. They told me it was over. I was all right. And then I went to sleep."

We gathered around her. A flat gray twilight was in the room. Dolores sat in the bed. Her long, dark tresses fell forward over her white shoulders.

My breath came fast. To see the light, form, color, the world, for the first time!

Very slowly, gently, Dr. Weatherby unwound the bandages. They dropped from his trembling hands to the bed.

"Now, Dolores, open you eyes, just a little."

The dark lashes on her cheeks fluttered up, and closed instantly against the light. She could see!

Her eyes opened again, timidly, fearfully. But they stayed open, glorious dark eyes, luminous eyes that were seeing! Eyes with light in them.

They opened very wide. Surprised, wondering!

"I see! I see!" There were no words to express her emotion. Just surprise and awe surging in her voice, stamped on her face. "I see! Jim, is that you, Jim? Why, that's Jim I see!" Her hand went to her eyes as thought to clear a blurring vision. "That . . . must be Jim. Come here, Jim. I want to see you closer."

He fell on his knees beside the bed, and her hands went to his shoulders, his face, his hair.

"Jim, it *is* you! It looks like you!"

"When do you suppose this king will see us, Len?" Jim asked. "How is Loro?"

"Oh, you weren't there when Ren told us. More to it than he said, of course, but that's none of our business and we're not going to make it our business. It was the end for Loro. It must have been planned that way."

"I surmised as much. It's pretty tough. At least he carried out his last wish and was able to make atonement for his crime by giving Dolores her sight. Now to our problem: I wish the king would see us. What did Ren say about that?"

I understood that our audience would be at any time. Ren was to let us know. Dolores had again fallen asleep. From where Jim and I sat I could see her bed, with Dr. Weatherby sitting there beside her.

Jim said, "When we once see the king and get out of here, things will look different. Why's the old doc sitting there so long? He acted queer to me, Len. Did you see his face when he knew that Dolores was cured?"

I never answered the question. We heard a sound from in there, a choking cry, and saw Dr. Weatherby with a hand clutching his throat.

"Len, what the infernal —"

We rushed in. Dr. Weatherby sat looking at us. He had torn the collar of his robe with convulsive fingers. He stared at us. His hands were groping for the sides of his chair. "Len! I can't . . . can't get up!"

Before we could reach him, his great head sagged to the high hunched shoulders. He twitched a little, then slumped inert.

I swung on Jim. "Go pound on the door! Tell them to let you out! Get Ren! Tell Ren to bring a doctor, someone to help us!"

"He's . . . dead?"

"No! Unconscious. He may be dying. Get help."

THEY BELIEVED THAT Dr. Weatherby was dying. He lay in a room off our main apartment now, still unconscious, lying with closed eyes, motionless save for the tiny stirring of his breath.

It was, by Earthly standards of day and night, now late afternoon, a soft, pale daylight. After another time of sleep the long night would be upon us.

They could not say how long Dr. Weatherby would live. There seemed nothing to do for him. The shock of his joy over Dolores, the let-down of the tension under which he had been laboring, had brought a collapse.

In hushed tones, with the awe of death upon us, we sat talking. We were on the upper half-story of the apartment off which the small bedrooms opened. I heard the sound of the door downstairs, and heard Ren's voice. "How is he?"

I leaned over the balcony. "There is no change. Come up, Ren."

He mounted the incline stairs. With him was a young girl. He introduced her gravely.

"The daughter of my uncle, who now is dead. She is named Sonya; she is very proud that she has learned from me your language. Hold out your hand, child. They shake it for the greeting, you see?"

I took the girl's extended hand. She was the first woman we had seen in this new realm, and I regarded her curiously. She seemed of an age before full maturity, a small girl, small as Dolores, slim, almost fragile of body, garbed in a single short garment from neck to knees.

It was a sort of smock, of soft dull-red pleats, gathered with a girdle at the waist, high at the neck, with long, tight-fitting sleeves to the waist. Over it was a long cloak of a heavier material which she discarded upon entering.

Her legs were bare. On her feet were leather sandals. Her hair was long and black as jet. Parted in the middle, it partially covered her ears, was caught by a thong at the back of her neck; and its long tresses, hanging nearly to her waist, were bound by a ribbon-like cord.

Her face was oval with expressive dark eyes and long black lashes. Sensuous lips, I thought, but a mouth and chin that bespoke a firm character. A beautiful young girl, intelligent, perhaps beyond most of her race. And that she was modish was plain to be seen.

Her coat had a jaunty cut to it, a lining of delicate fabric and contrasting color. Her smock was very tight at the throat, shoulders and sleeves, and tight across the bust to mould her youthful breasts.

It fell not quite to her knees and flared with a stiffly circular bottom. Her face carried the stamp of youth and health.

She discarded her cloak and stopped to remove the skin sandals from her feet. Upon her left leg, just above the knee, was clasped a broad, white metal band.

"I am glad to know the strangers." Her glance went to the room where Dr. Weatherby was lying. "But I intrude at a very sad time for you."

She and Ren sat quietly down among us. Ren said,

"Our king, too, is ill. A very old man." He shook his head dubiously.

"Oh," said Jim. "Well, then we —"

Sonya seemed to take the thought from him. "I have already told my cousin," she said quickly, "that you must swear your allegiance to the king at once. We need you. You men look very strong, very masterful."

She said it frankly, merely as a statement of fact, but there was an unconscious admiration in her gaze. "We need you and we . . . perhaps we need the girls." She said the last with a singular, enigmatic emphasis.

"Right," said Jim heartily. "You fix it up for us, get the audience. I want to be out of here. We've been tied here like timekeepers in a tower."

"Our king will die. That is sure now. Our girls must act; it is now or never!"

VIII

REBELLING VIRGINS

IT WAS FROM SONYA that we first learned any tangible details of this new realm. She and I, with Dolores and Alice, were seated by Dr. Weatherby's bedside. Two days had passed. His condition was unchanged. We were sure now that he would never regain consciousness.

The old king too, was more gravely ill than before. He had sent for us so that at his bedside we might take the oath of service. Jim had gone with Ren. The rest of us remained beside the dying doctor. The end would come soon, at any time now, doubtless.

Sonya was talking softly. I turned from the bedside to regard her earnest face.

"This city," she was saying, "we call Kalima. There was an ancient tribe dwelt here; the chief, they thought he was a god, the god Kali." She was addressing Alice, but now she turned to me. "Our land lies in a great depression of this globe's surface. Once, perhaps, it was the bottom of some great sea. It rises into mountains everywhere. It is not large; we are less than a quarter of a million people. The caves are at the foothills.

"You will hear more of them later." She had waved aside a question of Dolores'. "On the Great Island, not far from here, is what we call the Village of the Virgins, where now about three hundred girls are living in rebellion."

"Rebellion against the government?" I asked.

"Yes. Against the man-made laws." She smiled her quiet, grave smile. "You have come, you strangers, at a time to find our nation in what we girls think is a condition very grave. You, my friends, will understand very well what we girls are protesting against. And now, with our prince and princess vanished, and our king about to die, the time has come to —"

She checked herself suddenly.

Alice was regarding her with a blue-eyed gaze of quite obvious admiration. Dolores moved over on the low couch; her hand plucked at the hem of Sonya's smock as it lay just above her knees and touched the smooth white metal band that encircled her leg.

"Sonya, what is that? Just an ornament? It's very pretty."

"No," she said. "Not altogether for ornament. Every woman wears one." She brushed her fingers across it; her smile was quizzical. "It is, in fact, well . . . it had become almost a symbol of what we girls are striving for. The virgins' band. You see, it is quite unmarked. No man's name is engraved there. I'll explain in a moment.

"Our king, with twenty of his counselors — my cousin Ren is one of them — rule the nation. They make no new laws. The old laws are good enough for them. The guards, you would call them police, are all the army we have.

"They are all men, young, sturdy fellows who have no thought but to do what they are told. Which is right, of course. It is the laws which are wrong, inhuman. They are very old laws. They have now become customs, traditions, handed down from father to son."

Her tone was suddenly bitter. She gestured with a slim, expressive hand. "I must talk more calmly. These things against which we have now come to open rebellion, were doubtless necessary at the beginning. The laws were made by men who knew no better.

"The difficulty is in the sex of our children. Out of three births, two on the average are females and only one a male. We have, therefore, twice as many females as males — twice as many women as men. Or at least, there would be twice as many if —" She checked herself again.

"Thus we have . . . I think Ren said that on Earth it was termed polygamy. A man may marry more than one woman."

Dolores said impulsively, "Oh, I would not like that! It used to be a custom in many parts of the Earth, but there is almost none of it now."

"We girls of this generation do not like it either," said Sonya.

Her voice turned very grave. "What we are rebelling against is far worse. Often our girl children, if they seem not destined to be beautiful, are killed. The father does not wish the expense of too many girls.

"Girls or women are never allowed to work. They must only strive to be beautiful. And when they have at last reached the proper age, to get rid of them by marriage, the father must pay a large tax to the state.

"At the age of twenty a girl must choose one of the men who has recorded his name as desiring her. Any man is legally eligible to do that. He may have no wife as yet. Or he may have one wife, or several. If he has the necessary money for the tax, and deposits it with the government, his name is recorded.

"You see," she was cynical now, "the government needs the money. And it likes our girls to be beautiful. Fifty men may record their names as desiring a girl who is very beautiful.

"She can choose but one man. But the government only refunds half the money the others have deposited. It makes a lot of money on a very beautiful girl."

"A sort of lottery!" I exclaimed. "With women as the prizes."

"I do not understand," said Sonya. "But that is the way it is with us. Beautiful girls are profitable to the government. No girl-child who showed promise of beauty has ever been found murdered.

"But woman's beauty fades, and there are many female mouths to feed, and female bodies to clothe and house. It make more work for the men and the men do not like to work. And so —"

The cynicism had left her voice. A hush fell upon her tragic words. "And so, when a woman can no longer bear children, when her beauty is going, then she is considered a burden.

"She has never been trained to work. She is useless; an expense.

"Each year our old women are chosen — a certain number of them, depending on the birth-rate — are chosen to die. They are given a blanket, a little food, and are taken to the place we call Death Island. Left there alone, they live a while. Then die.

"I've seen them draw the death number! I've seen, on the island, their wasted bodies lying huddled!" Her voice choked. "But they go away, start for the island so patient, so resigned.

"It is that for which we are in rebellion more than anything else! We of this generation now cannot stand it. We will not stand it!"

To my mind had come memories of the savages of our Earth, not so many centuries ago. They too, had thought it expedient to leave aged members of their tribes to die. The vision Sonya was invoking to my imagination was horrible. I found my voice.

"Your men here, Sonya, surely they are not all against you girls? Your cause?"

"No," she said. "But how many are with us at heart, we do not know. And men are very strange. You cannot talk with them; they pretend you are not intelligent enough to be worthy of talking. My cousin Ren —"

Ren! It seemed incongruous.

She went on. "He is like all the rest. It is not, from his viewpoint, inhuman. It is the way things always have been. His mother died that way. He says, 'Her life was ended.' He says that men, brave men, meet death that way. Their life is over, the creator calls them and they go bravely."

"But," said Dolores, "the man who hands out the death number is not the creator."

"Ah," said Sonya, "but if you told that to a man he would say you do not understand."

Her hand went to her leg. "You asked me about this band. It is placed upon us when we are just maturing. On it is engraved the man we are to marry.

"If he divorces us, that is written here, and the name of the man who next takes us. Our marriage record: written plain that all may see!" Her fingers touched the band's smooth surface. "There is nothing on mine, as yet. And there never will be, unless we win our case."

Alice said, "Are you one of the rebels?"

"I am at heart, and I'm working with them. Technically, I am not. It is nearly a year yet, as you on your Earth measure time, before I am of the age when I can be forced to marry."

"What have the girls done?" I asked. "Refused to marry?"

"Yes. About eighteen hundred of them. Most are just about at the legal age. They left the cities, went to the Great Island, and there they have built themselves a village. They grow food there; they work; they are self-supporting. To many old women and a few girl-children, they have given sanctuary."

"And the government does nothing about it?" I exclaimed.

"They did, at first. Men were sent to the Virgins' Island to get some of the old women; but the girls forcibly resisted them. Some of the girls were killed. Nothing much has been done about it since. The government, I think, does not know what to do."

She was scornful. "Our girls are very beautiful. It would not be profitable to kill them."

Alice said, "You reach the marriage age in a year, Sonya? Have any men recorded their names for you?"

"Oh, yes," she said. "There were eight, I think, when I last went to the records."

"But you wouldn't marry any of them? Or perhaps I should not ask."

"Why not? There is no secret in such things. One man whose name is recorded for me I love very dearly. Our prince."

A sound from Dolores interrupted her. Dolores was sitting with hands to her forehead and eyes closed. She murmured, "I caught someone's thoughts! Now they come again."

We waited through a breathless silence. Then Dolores muttered, "The prince. You called him Altho? It is he!"

Sonya gripped her. "What is he thinking? Tell me! Tell me quickly!"

Then she too, received the thoughts. She sat tense. "Oh, the princess is dead! Killed!"

"Killed!" echoed Dolores. Then her face went vague: she was getting nothing more.

But evidently Sonya was still in communication. She cried aloud involuntarily, "Altho! Dearest, dearest Altho! Where are you? Tell Sonya. Oh, he does not know! Or he cannot tell me! He says — " it was a stark whisper of horror — "he says soon he will be killed too."

She sprang to her feet, then abruptly sat down again. "Altho! Altho, where are you?"

The communication broke. Her face went vague, puzzled, empty. And then despairing.

Beyond the window, in the street below the balcony, a sudden murmur of voices floated up to us. We went to the balcony. It was night now, a night of pale stars in a cloudless sky. Shouting people were coming up the street. They appeared in a moment at the bottom of the hill, a crowd of men, a hundred or more. They came forward, swept around the corner, and vanished. Above the babble was a single sentence. A man called it. Others took it up.

Sonya murmured, "They say, 'Our king is dying.' And the princess is dead! And your grandfather . . . Death everywhere!"

The man in the street shouted again. And Sonya sprang from the couch.

"He says, 'Our king is dead.'" She laughed hysterically. "Death everywhere! I must go to the virgins. Will you come? I can take you. The virgins are ready! We must act at once!"

IX

THE NAMELESS HORROR

I T WAS THE FIRST TIME we had any freedom since our arrival. Ren had not returned with Jim. If the king were really dead, there would be a great confusion at the castle. They might be detained indefinitely.

Sonya would not wait. "A few hours only," she urged. "Then we will be back. I will leave a message for my cousin and your friend."

The first shock of Dr. Weatherby's death was over. There was no advantage in the girls remaining here.

We started finally. On the lower floor of the house we found long dark cloaks and donned them, with a queerly flat, mound-shaped hat for me and light scarves to cover the girls' heads. The lower door was open. Ren had left it so, knowing that Sonya would stay with us.

Technically we were prisoners. But Sonya paid scant cere-mony to that now. The king was dead: our oath of allegiance to the nation would be taken for granted.

"My allegiance goes to you," Dolores said naively. "You girls."

Alice nodded.

"Yes," said Sonya. "But do not say so openly. And you, my friend, Leonard — you are a man — be careful what you say if you have any sympathy for our cause."

Sympathy! How mild a word, as again visions of what she had told us sprang before me!

In this residential section of the city there was at this hour no traffic in the street. The shouting crowd had disappeared. Sonya led us to the main street level. The pedestrian bridges were above us.

An unnatural silence seemed to hang about the dark, somnolent city, as though it only seemed sleeping and was wide awake. A tenseness was in the air. The houses were dark, but in almost every window I fancied that figures were watching, faces peering out.

We avoided the lights. Mounted the hill for a block or two, then turned into a very narrow street of shadows.

The houses here, the back of houses, I assumed, were blank, two-story walls.

We passed each of them hurriedly. My heart was thumping. Sonya had said that these were merely back entrances to inner courtyards of the houses. But it seemed, to my sharpened fancy, that in every one some horrible lurking thing was waiting to spring upon us.

Sonya was leading. She was taking us through a back way to her home, to get the vehicle that would transport us to the island. We were nearing the end of the alley; it opened ahead of us into a broad street with a dim glow of light illuminating it. To our right, just ahead, was a courtyard entrance: a yawning cave-mouth of emptiness.

We had almost reached it when Sonya abruptly halted, checked our advance as though she had struck some invisible barrier, stopped, and shrank backward, pressing against us. And her hand in terror was over her mouth to stifle a scream.

I saw it then, what she was seeing. A thing, something monstrous, lurking in the blackness of that cave-like house entrance, a thing huge, of vague, grotesque outline, an upright thing, with a great balloon-like head, bobbing from side to side, two eyes glowing in the darkness. And below them, where a neck might have been, two other smaller eyes, green, blazing points of fire.

In all my veins the blood seemed freezing, prickling needle-points of ice exuding through my pores, my scalp prickling at the hair-roots. I was stricken with fright and horror. But an instinct, so that I scarcely realized what I was doing, made me pull Sonya soundlessly backward, sweep all three of the girls behind me and downward. And as they sank to the pavement, I crouched tense in front of them.

The thing seemingly had not heard us, or seen us. It advanced out of the darkness of the doorway; in the dimness of the outside light I saw it more clearly, a thing like a great upright animal, ten feet tall, perhaps, and monstrously cast in human mold, with thick, bent legs. It had a long, thick trunk with wide, powerful shoulders and a deep, bulging chest, and arms that dangled nearly to its knees.

Its head, no wider than its powerful neck, was small, round, and flat on top. There seemed a face; its tiny blazing eyes were plain in the darkness.

A two-headed thing! The smaller head was bent forward. Behind it, as though astride of the shoulders, was another head, balloon-like: huge, wider than the shoulders, a head seemingly inflated, distended. A large flat face. The thing took a step. Its larger head wobbled as it moved.

My hand behind me kept the girls motionless. The thing came to the end of the narrow street, emerged into the glow of light there. It did not pause — the light obviously was not to its liking — it bounded sidewise, noiseless on padded feet, and was gone into the shadows.

But in that instant under the light, I had seen it more clearly. A giant, gorilla-like figure. A man! Black hair seemed upon its body, but the body was partially clothed. And I fancied I had seen a belt strapped about its waist, with dangling weapons.

The bobbling head astride its shoulder was very different from the rest of the thing. A bloated membrane? I got that impression. It seemed a smooth, dead-white skin; I thought I had seen distended veins on it.

And as the powerful body leaped, I fancied I saw thin little arms, four of them, hanging inert from the bloated head.

It was gone. I breathed again. Behind me the huddled girls were shuddering. At my ear Sonya was whispering,

"The Nameless Horror!"

X

THE FLIGHT TO THE VIRGINS' ISLAND

WE DID NOT continue down the street. Sonya took us back. We turned another corner, and another. Soon we were near her home. She had not swerved from her purpose to take us to the Virgins' Island. This thing we had seen was one of many of its kind which dwelt in the fastnesses of the mountains beyond the caves.

They never came out into the light; none, Sonya thought, had ever been seen more clearly than we had seen this one. No man of this realm, to Sonya's knowledge, had ever ventured into the caves to seek them out.

I could not understand such a condition. On Earth, nothing had ever been so fearsome but that man had sought to destroy it. But these people were of a different cast of mind.

"Sonya," I demanded, "how long have these things been in the caves?"

"They were first seen only just before our prince and princess vanished."

We reached Sonya's home, a low, oval stone building, dark in its enshrouding garden of flower-trees. She led us aside, toward a small outbuilding. I suddenly paused.

I was in sympathy with Sonya and her cause, but was not the plight of the prince more important? Had I not better go and join Jim now, and follow the course we had planned?

We reached the dark, single-storied outbuilding. Sonya touched a switch. A soft glow showed inside. It was a square building of stone and metal, windows barred by a metal screening, a doorway with a hinged screen.

"Sonya," I said, "just what is this you intend doing?"

She regarded me. Alice and Dolores stood beside her. I found myself arrayed against the three of them.

"Why," she said, "we are going to the Island of the Virgins. The girls are ready; we have been waiting —" she hesitated, then finished, "waiting for this chance which has come tonight."

"What chance? The king being ill or dead?"

Her eyes flashed. "Yes. The girls are ready. They will come back with us, now."

She stood with shoulders squared, a defiant little figure before us.

I said, more gently, "What are you girls planning to do, Sonya?"

I think she had already told Alice and Dolores. They moved closer as though to defend her. Alice flashed me a defiant look.

I repeated, "What are you planning to do?"

Her eyes held level. "It is not my secret. You are a man. I have no right to tell you." She added very slowly, but wholly without emotion,

"I think perhaps you had better go back."

It struck me with a vague sense of shame. I felt like a deserter.

Alice said calmly, "Are you going back, Len?"

With what loyalty these girls already were banded against me! Little Dolores clutched me.

"Don't do that, Leonard! Sonya, you misunderstand him."

I tried to explain myself. "It's only because I thought the other course would be better for the prince," I finished. "How long will this take us, Sonya?"

Sudden tears were in her eyes. "I believe you! But you must know that I . . . least of all, would delay to help him I love! Mine is the better way, and we won't be long — a few hours at most."

I yielded, "All right, Sonya. You know best."

We entered the building, a large room divided by the metal screening into huge cages. A great commotion, the flapping of wings, greeted our entrance. Travel in this realm was indeed primitive. We were to go by air, on a gliding platform drawn by giant birds trained to harness.

Sonya pulled down a swinging tube of light from the ceiling and held it toward one of the cages. Eight giant birds were there, soft, gray-white feathered bodies, heads small, round and bald with black top-knots like plumes.

They stood upon short legs, yet were as tall as myself. They seemed very gentle; they regarded us timorously, but curiously. They knew Sonya; as she entered the cage, they nuzzled with their beaks against her smock.

"Ah, Nana! They want sweets," she laughed. One, more bold, pecked at her pocket. She leaned, and with her shoulder heaved it away. Then she produced small pieces of sweetmeat and made them each take a piece decorously.

"They are well trained, you see?" She rested an arm against the great curving side of one of them. I could well imagine that on its soft back she could have ridden into the air. One had lazily opened its wings; a feathered spread of fifteen feet at least, graceful wings, gray-white, with tips that were solid black.

The platform was under an enclosure of the flat roof. Sonya rolled it out, a platform some ten feet long, by six wide. Soft furs covered its surface. It was mounted upon small wheels, with a frame set in small cylinders of compressed gas as cushions against the shock of landing.

Midway of the platform, underneath, was a cross rod. Sonya extended its sections sidewise, each jutting out some six feet beyond the platform edge. To each of the ends of this rod, a bird was harnessed. The other six were in two strings in front, three in a string, one in advance of the other.

There were reins for the leading birds to pull their heads gently from one side to the other, a rein to pull downward on their feet, another rein, which when drawn upon, raised a cushion to press upward against the bird's throat.

It took Sonya only a few minutes to harness them. I had been inspecting the platform. It was built of a light metal framework, upon which a thin, strong membrane was stretched. The whole seemed light as a kite.

Beneath it, set in the space between its landing gear, was a system of small, flexible wings, and moveable cones through which the air rushed. And there was a horizontal and vertical rudder, with flexible tips. Flying skill was needed. There were several controls near the front of the platform, where now the reins were held in a notched crossbar.

"We are ready," said Sonya. She stretched upon her side on the fur covering of the platform with the reins and the controls before her.

We took our places beside her and behind her, lying at full

length, arms crooked into leather straps to hold us. Sonya called to the birds. Eight of them as one, leaped upward. The great wings flapped. We moved, rolled across the roof. At its edge we lifted with a jerk.

The low housetop, the dark trees, other roofs, the dim city lights all slid downward into a blue of shadow. On a long slant, we headed upward into the starlit night.

I lay on my side, clinging to that swaying, leaping platform. The wind surged past, tearing away every sound save the flapping of those giant wings. A graceful bird on each side of me, two strings of them slanting upward in front, winged swiftly up into the night, drawing me after them.

The dark world was lost and gone. The star-encrusted dome of the heavens encompassed everything.

This was not an air voyage. It was flying. The platform fluttered, slid over the air like some swiftly drawn kite. The heavens swung with a dizzy lurching. I gazed over the edge at the dark, moving landscape far down.

The faint lights of the city showed a thinly-built, suburban area, then the shore of a star-lit sea ahead. Primitive flying, with the first startling strangeness of it gone, its romance swept over me, a magic carpet upon which I lay, magically flying over realms of mystery, a flight unreal — romantically miraculous.

I was brought back from roaming fancy. Dolores, lying beside me, was pulling at my shoulder. I caught her words before the wind snatched at them.

"Look, Leonard! There is the island!"

There was no fear of this flight upon Dolores's face. Only an eager wonderment, her mind struggling with these sights: romantic, awing to me, how much more so to her so newly emerged from a lifelong darkness! "See the island, Leonard?"

We were, I suppose, no more than a thousand feet high. The shore of the sea was nearly beneath us, a dark, curving shore of gray sand with gentle white waves rolling upon it. Beyond the shore, some ten miles out, a dark island showed. It seemed irregularly circular.

As we swept closer its beach became visible, gray-white sand with white rollers. A tangle of vegetation was behind the beach, a forest jungle with the land sloping up over gentle foothills to a cone-shaped hill which occupied the island's center.

Along one shore of the island, yellow and blue spots of lights were showing among the trees at the edge of the beach. It was all dim in the starlight. Far ahead, where the sea unbroken reached the horizon of stars, a yellow glow had come to the sky.

Sonya gestured, "The Moon is rising."

It came with a startling abruptness. A great yellow world swung up, twice, three times the visual size of our moon: a glowing yellow disk, marked with the dark configurations of its mountains. It rose horn-shaped, mounted straight up, slowly, but with a movement quite visible. The stars paled around it. A flood of yellow light lay upon the sea in a broad path of rippling gold.

The island was bathed in the golden flood. We were much closer to it now, swooping a few hundred feet above its beach which along here was broad and hard. The jungle was beside us, a fairyland of tropical verdure.

Warmed by the waters of the sea, and perhaps by hidden fires of the cone-shaped hill, the vegetation grew to giant size.

A giant forest edged with gold, mysteriously dark, romantic, amorous, scented with spices and the heavy perfume of flowers.

We landed upon the beach where the warm waves were liquid gold beside low, primitive, palm-thatched dwellings set like ground nests in the verdure.

With the rush of our flight gone, I felt a new warmth in the air. Upon my cheeks was the caressing breath of a warm breeze from the sea; it stirred the palm-fronds to amorous whispering.

White figures were drawn back from the beach to watch us land. They crowded forward into the moonlight, young girls, slim and white, with long, flowing black hair.

As I stood up and stepped from the platform to the sand, some of them scattered and fled with startled feminine cries into the enshrouded foliage. Others came shyly forward, crowded around us — golden nymphs in the moonlight, with a brief, veil-like garment from shoulder to thigh.

They were surprised at me, a man, here upon their island, They crowded around Sonya, talking seemingly all at once, casting mistrustful glances at me, and glances of curiosity and friendliness at Alice and Dolores.

What Sonya said to them I could only guess. It caused an excitement; like fauns, many of them leaped away, running down the beach, scattering over the village. In the distance I could hear their cries, and other cries, shouts, a great activity beginning.

And presently there was heard the cheep of giant birds, the

flapping of their wings as they were released from their cages and brought out to be harnessed. Far ahead down the beach in the moonlight, presently a crowd of the girls began rolling out a huge platform.

The few girls who remained with Sonya continued talking. They were tense now, but wholly composed, beautiful, intelligent-looking girls, most of them a year or so older than Sonya, and very much the same type. Upon the left leg of each, just above the knee, was a broad metal band.

The girls now were ignoring me. But Sonya called Dolores and Alice over, and it was obvious they were welcomed.

I saw presently, some of the older women. With a few little girls among them, they came to the edge of the forest and stood timidly regarding us — infancy and age, common fugitives.

Alice was gesturing toward the sky. I turned. Off there in the starlight, in the direction we had come, was a lone bird flying. In a moment I could see its wings.

Sonya called something; and added to Alice, "A girl arriving from Kalima."

The bird swooped in a great descending arc, a great white bird like those which had drawn our platform. Mounted upon its back was the figure of a girl, her arms clinging about its neck. It soared with poised wings, descended to the beach near us.

The girl leaped to the sand and called, "Sonya! Sonya!"

They talked in their own language; then Sonya whirled to me. Her face had gone white.

"Alta, the girl, lives very near Ren's house in Kalima. I do not mean my home, his and mine. I mean that other house of his where you were living. Alta went there to see me."

She was talking swiftly. Alice and Dolores drew me to one side; a common feeling of disaster was upon us all.

"Alta found the door open and went in. She read my message to Ren, that we had come here to the island. She was leaving. In the street outside she heard voices. From the window she saw Ren and your Jim. They were nearly to the house.

"Then . . . a great black thing leaped upon them, a giant, with a great, wobbling head. What we saw, Leonard! The Nameless Horror! It leaped upon them, and there were two or three others of its kind. They seized my cousin and Jim. Lifted them up, carried them off! She . . . Alta, took one of my birds, and came here to tell us!"

XI

A MAN, TO PLAY A MAN'S PART

I STOOD A MOMENT, transfixed with horror. Alice's face had become as white as Sonya's. Dolores uttered a faint little cry, "Jim!"

"Sonya —" I began. But she had turned to give orders to the girls. They sped away. I finished, "Sonya, get me back, at once!"

"Yes," she agreed. "But you can do nothing — a stranger — you cannot talk our language."

"I can, with you to interpret for me."

She whirled upon Alta with other questions, then back to me. "More than ever now, I must got through with our plans. Alta says the king is not dead, but dying; he will die at any moment. We must get back."

Down the beach the large platform was ready. A hundred girls or more were loading upon it. With a great flapping of the wings of the birds, it moved down the beach. Rose into the air. It had four strings of ten birds each, with others harnessed in tandem all along its sides. Magnificently, it sailed upward, turned in a broad arc, and passed us high overhead.

From everywhere now the girls were rising. Another great platform, and still another. A score of smaller ones; and from the forest, a hundred or more individual birds, each with a lone rider.

They flapped up from among the palms; circled overhead, with their numbers augmenting until they headed away. The first platforms were now mere blobs in the starlight. A thousand girls, I estimated, were up there in flight.

We hurried to our platform. Again we were in the air. Below us still another platform was rising; around us, three or four mounted birds circled like a convoy. We took our place in the line and sped back to the city.

"Is the king dead, Sonya?"

"No. I do not think so."

I waited a moment. "Sonya, you girls are not armed?"

She said impulsively, "No. But in the underground rooms of the castle, the science weapons are stored. Once we get control of them —" She checked herself, but she had told me what I wanted to know. An arsenal under the castle! The weapons of a half-forgotten science of this decadent race, stored there!

I shuddered at the visions which surged to my imagination. Here in the city — a government menaced by crusading girls! This was our condition, pitiable indeed, to oppose a savage, outside enemy!

Yet what was I to do? I pondered it until a vague possibility came to me. It gripped me. It seemed feasible. I believed I could accomplish it. With swiftness of action, power, dominance, I could carry it through. A grim exaltation was upon me. A man, to play a man's part.

We landed with a swoop upon the moonlit garden sward. The girls crowded around us, with a fringe of curious, apathetic men behind them. Sonya turned to speak to Alice and Dolores. Nearby was a dark path between beds of giant flowers. I slipped from the platform. With my cloak held before my face, I avoided the girls and plunged into the shadows of the flowered path.

The path was dark, cut off from the moonlight by a great bed of flowers rising high above my head. A group of men came toward me; I slipped between the flower stalks, stood enshrouded in my cloak, my figure merging with the shadows, until the men had passed.

I caught a near glimpse of them. Young men, stalwart fellows, no doubt, according to the standards of their race. But not one of them was taller than my shoulder, and beside me, they were frail, delicate of build.

In a weaponless fight, I could doubtless have engaged two or three of them, and come off the victor.

The path turned into a dim street that encircled the rear of the castle, into the arsenal through some postern gate along here. The arsenal was within this curving wall of stone. I passed such a gate now, a small narrow opening, half the height of my upright body. But it was blocked solidly with a metal door which I could see no way of opening.

I passed on, heading back through the city to the house in which we had been held since our arrival. Behind the house, with a viaduct connecting them, was the laboratory room in which we had arrived. Our space-vehicle was there. I could not operate the vehicle, but it held a weapon I wanted.

I remembered that Jim had brought it. In the excitement of our arrival, the strangeness of everything, we had forgotten it, the Frazier beam, brought out by an Aberdeen physicist in 1994.

I had left the castle behind me, and turned, somewhat dubiously, into another street. I was sure if I could get to Sonya's house, where so recently we had been, I could retrace my way from there. I had planned this while on the flying platform as we circled the castle. I had been able then to locate Sonya's home, and to gauge the lay of the streets in between. I turned another corner. The street was brighter.

Another corner. I saw and recognized Sonya's house. From there, my way was sure. Within twenty minutes after leaving the castle grounds, I was groping in the darkness back of the house where Dr. Weatherby's body lay.

It was near here that the Nameless Horror had caught Jim and Ren. But I saw no signs of them now. The viaduct connecting the two buildings was a dark thin line against the stars. The building I was hoping to enter was wholly dark. A two-story structure: the viaduct extended from its upper floor.

I prowled around. The lower window openings were all barred. The door oval was barred. A stairway led up from the ground to the viaduct. From the viaduct's platform I saw a cornice, too high for a normal man to reach. But I leaped for it, pulled myself up upon the dome-shaped roof of a turret.

A leap from here and I was upon the main flat roof. There should be a door under a mound cover; most of the buildings had them. I located it, wrenched at its bar. It yielded. I went down a curving metal ladder, into the house. In a moment I had located the laboratory room. Our vehicle in its full normal size lay here, dead white, an end of it tinged yellow by a shaft of moonlight.

I stepped within it, went to Jim's cupboard, lighting a tiny battery light overhead. The Frazier weapon I sought was here.

Its *copite* cone, with smooth glistening bone handle, *copite* head-band, they tiny pulse motor, the wires; it was all complete.

A triumph swept me. I was unarmed no longer. Playing a long hand, here in this strange world, a man, comparatively of giant strength and physical power. But I was more than that now. I had a mental weapon, and the mental strength to use it.

I did not stop to adjust the apparatus. I wound it up in its wire, and hastily retreated. I reached the street, with the weapon under my cloak. I hurried back to the castle over the same route; I did not want to chance losing my way.

But as I advanced, I had more than memory of the streets to guide me. From the direction of the castle, a blur of cries was audible, a hum, a murmur, which as I progressed resolved itself into shouts. The shouting of a mob: heavy, angry voices of men, shrill cries of girls, a single, long, agonized scream of a girl.

I was on a lower street that fronted the water. A side entrance to the castle grounds was before me. Through the trees I could see the frowning, turreted walls of the castle. I stopped to adjust my weapon.

It took no more than a moment. Around my forehead, with hat discarded, I bound the headband, a narrow strip of finely woven *copite* wire, with two small electrodes pressing my temples.

On the right side two finely drawn, silk-insulated wires dangled from the headband to my neck. I tucked them under my shirt, over my shoulder, down my right arm to my wrist. A band at my wrist, to which the wires were attached, held the tiny pulse-motor in place. My heart set it in motion, to generate the necessary current.

The Frazier projector was a *copite* cone, this one some ten inches long; its shape was a cone section, one end, the muzzle, with an open diameter of six inches, the other end, one-fifth inch, across which the diaphragm was fitted.

The bone handle screwed into place at the diaphragm. It was hollow. Within it were amplifying tubes and a transformer, miracles of smallness. The whole projector weighed some twenty Troy ounces. I pulled the two connecting wires from my wrist-band to its butt, gripped the handle with my index finger along its side, resting on the trigger button.

I was ready! My heart was racing. The tiny motor at my wrist was racing. I could feel the hum of the current, the prickling of it under the forehead band, its tiny stabbing throb at the electrodes pressing my temples. There was power within me.

I had flung off my cloak. I stood in the white silk shirt, dark, short, tight trousers, and high, heavy black stockings of my Earth costume, stood with outflung arms for an instant and exulted in the wave of triumph which swept me. Against these people the power of my weapon would be invincible.

Furtive no longer, I advanced with bold, open strides to the gate of the castle grounds. A few men were there, evidently about to enter. They stared at me. Before the strangeness of my aspect, the boldness of my flashing glance, they quailed, cried with fear and scattered before me.

I did not heed them. Beyond the gate, back from the water there was a rise of ground. I mounted it, and from the thicket of flowers that ornamented its top, gazed out at the moonlit scene.

Between the mound on which I stood, and the foot of the broad staircase leading up the broad terrace to the castle entrance, a throng of men were standing.

Spectators, standing idle. Occasionally a group of them would surge forward in one direction or the other, milling about some individual who seemed abruptly determined upon a course of action. A mob without a leader. Excited, aimless, striving for points of vantage to see what was taking place in front.

The girls were massed at the foot of the castle steps. Evidently, just before I arrived, the girls had tried to mount them. The guards were gathered in a group on top. Half way down, a girl's body was lying. It writhed, rolled down the steps. From the crowd of men a murmur rose.

The scene was clear in the yellow moon-glow. The throng of girls at the staircase bottom were gathering their leaders, preparing again to mount. The tense guards on top seemed confused, not knowing how to deal with this unarmed attack.

On the castle balcony, at the head of the steep metal stairway, a few other guards were standing. And on the rooftop, I could make out the doddering figures of old men, gazing down in confused terror.

There was, momentarily, a pause over the scene; a silence, expectant.

But abruptly the hush was broken by a shrill, electrical whine. It rose in pitch to a scream, a siren from the castle battlements. It screamed for a moment, then abruptly was stilled.

I wondered what it meant. The crowd was stricken breathless. But for an instant only. Then it broke into a roar of shouting.

The king had died!

I did not know it at the time, but I suspected it. On the rooftop, the old men were waving their arms; one of them seemed trying to talk to the throng. But his voice was lost in the din.

As though the siren had been a signal, the girls began swarming up the staircase, unarmed girls — unarmed save for the shining armor of their virginity and the desperation of their purpose. I stood watching; it was necessary for me to know with what arms the guards were equipped.

Some fifty young men, they stood in a group at the head of the staircase. The girls came up in a throng. I saw then that each of the guards seemed armed only with a long, curved knife, like a scimitar, incased in a black metal sheath.

Some drew these knives, waved the naked blades. But the girls were beyond intimidation. They came surging — a hundred of them in the first rank, with other hundreds pressing from below. The guards met them halfway down, a confusion of white figures with the black forms of the guards struggling in their midst.

A man with twenty girls around him. He did not want to use his naked sword. It was torn from him, the girls tearing at him savagely. He went down; the white forms swept over him. A girl had secured his sword waved it with shrill cries.

Another guard, more desperate, was using his sheathed weapon as a club. He had cleared a space around him. A girl leaped; the club struck her head. She fell limp. But he too, was soon overwhelmed.

The girls presently were near the staircase top; the guards remaining there were standing now, all with naked swords. I could not doubt that they would be driven to use them. The girls momentarily had paused, a dozen steps below them.

Many now were armed with swords they had taken. The blades were waving. A score of girls with the swords pushed their way to the upper rank, gathered for concerted, frenzied action. Then, with a rush, started up the empty intervening steps.

I had been standing on that hillock, enshrouded by the flowers. I had wanted to be sure beyond a doubt, how the guards were armed, and had hoped vainly that I might locate Sonya. And a fear had struck me for Alice and Dolores. Where were they in all this turmoil?

I thought I saw Sonya now, her white-limbed figure, with the dark, high-necked smock. She was creeping along up the steep bank of the terrace beside the staircase, trying, no doubt, to attain the top unnoticed, and thus to surprise the guards from behind.

My time had come. I stepped from the shadows of the flowers into a broad patch of moonlight. From the hillock here, I knew my figure would be visible from all parts of the scene. I stood, drawn to full height, with arms outstretched. And called with all my voice,

"Sonya! Sonya!"

The fighting did not stop, but the nearer men of the crowd turned and saw me. A murmur went up.

"Sonya! Sonya! Sonya!"

I kept repeating it. The murmur spread; rose to a shouting, shouts of wonderment, awe, and then fear. I strove to hold my voice to dominate the noise.

"Sonya! Sonya! Sonya!"

The faces were turning my way. The shouting near me died into a frightened silence. The men were milling about, with a surge away from me. Over on the stairs I saw the girls had paused in their attack.

"Sonya! Sonya! Sonya!"

She had turned, was staring at me. I waved my arms.

"Sonya! I am Leonard; come here!"

I plunged forward down the hillock path. The crowd scattered before me.

"Sonya, come here!"

She had turned. She was coming! I advanced steadily, not running, walking swiftly, with arms outstretched, menacing the crowd with my unknown weapon. The throng was stricken motionless with the strangeness of my aspect. From the staircase, the girls were staring; the guards were staring, a sea of faces, everywhere staring.

Calmly I advanced, and before me now a lane opened in the crowd. For all my outward calmness, my heart was pounding.

The pulse-motor at my wrist was throbbing. I had not used my weapon yet. But it would be effective.

"Sonya! Come here! Hurry! Sonya!"

My words, strange of language, awed the crowd further. The men parted before Sonya's running figure. She came up panting, white-faced.

"Len!"

"Sonya, you are going to obey me! You understand? You . . . everyone — obey me."

She stared. I was speaking swiftly, grimly, imperatively. "You stay at my side. I'll want you to translate when I give orders. Was that siren to announce the king's death?"

"Yes, he . . . Leonard, what are you doing? That thing in your hand —"

I silenced her. And then, fearing perhaps that she might not follow me, I gripped her hand, jerked her forward as I ran with rapid strides toward the crowd of girls at the foot of the stairway.

I think that Sonya believed at that moment that I had lost my reason. Her face stared up at me with terror in her eyes — a frightened child beside my bulk, whom I was dragging forward so swiftly that she could hardly keep her feet.

A few men near us shouted to me, but when I turned ferociously on them, they ran. Someone threw a missile at me, then another — stones which they were picking up from the flower-beds. One struck my back; and one struck Sonya.

The crowd was beginning to take courage; a wave of it surged at me. Struggling men shoving one another, shouted menacingly at me; but the men in the front rank, shoved forward by the press behind them, were pushing back, away from me.

Another stone hit me. I stopped short. I did not want to use the Frazier beam yet — time enough for that.

"Sonya, tell them to stop!" I dropped my hand, stood away from her. "Tell them that I won't hurt you! Tell them to stop . . . or I'll kill them! All of them!"

The missiles stopped at the first sound of my voice. From the stairway top a guard was shouting up to one of the old men on the roof; at Sonya's voice they both were silent to listen.

I added swiftly, "Sonya, you follow me! I don't want to drag you! Will you come?"

"Yes. I . . . I'll come."

I took her at her word and ran on. I had overawed an

unarmed crowd of spectators. But the girls were still ahead of me, a thousand or more of them, jammed near the foot of the great stairway, and a hundred or two more upon it.

I reached the first of them, with Sonya running fleet as a faun behind me. The girls, unarmed, scattered to give us room. We dashed through to the foot of the stairway, began mounting it.

The girls on it made way for me. But, halfway up, I saw above me, three girls with swords. They stood their ground, and whirled to oppose me.

Others with swords were near them and turned at me also, and above them, I was aware that the guards were coming down from the top to attack them from behind.

I stopped, and thrust Sonya in front of me. "You tell your girls to get out of the way!"

She screamed it.

"Again, Sonya! Tell them to get off the stairway! Fools! Can't they understand I'm here for them! Get them off here, I tell you! I'll handle those guards up there!"

It stung Sonya into action. She shouted my commands, rushed up a few steps, waving the girls aside. Behind me, they were retreating, clearing the stairway. Above they stood undecided, with awkwardly brandished swords, undecided whether to oppose me or to turn to defend themselves from the guards coming down from above.

Then one girl came, passing me hurriedly along the edge of the broad steps, then another. Then they all came with a rush.

And presently the stairs above me were empty, up to near the top where the guards had retreated and now stood with drawn swords gazing down at me. Empty steps, save for a girl's white body lying head down in a crimson pool.

I started slowly up. "Keep behind me, Sonya — careful! You'll be safe enough."

In silence I mounted toward the line of swords. The guards stood a moment in doubt. Then from the castle roof one of the old men screamed a command. The guards answered it. With a leap they came surging down the top steps to rush me.

I raised the Frazier muzzle, pressed its trigger. Its pale-green beam sprang out through the moonlight. I waved it lightly, and it spread, painting the oncoming guards with its thin, lurid color.

The first of them fell; his sword clattered; his body came hurtling down. I swept Sonya aside to avoid it.

Another fell, but held to a step, lying huddled. Two more sank to their hands and knees, stiffened, awkwardly propped against the steps.

A dozen more were standing frozen of movement, with swords held stiffly outstretched. And a few retreated woodenly to the top level where they stood swaying drunkenly, stupidly regarding me, hypnotized by the power of my will which the Frazier beam had intensified and thrown at them.

I snapped off he beam. Its effect, with my flashing glance to aid it, would last five minutes or more.

Hypnotized in the modern sense, very much as the ancients claimed they could do it with the eyes alone, and mysterious passes of the hands, these men here now, to some extent, would do my bidding. Certainly, they were powerless to move, save as I might direct them.

I swung to Sonya. "They're not hurt! Not injured! Tell the crowd; tell everyone it's an evidence of power."

Down in the garden the throng was pouring out the gates in a panic, hundreds milling at the gates, trying to escape. They quieted somewhat at the sound of Sonya's shrill voice.

We mounted past the stricken guards. They moved slightly; they were recovering. At the top, I stood, and with vehement thoughts commanded them to move aside. They swayed, moved a few steps, like sleepwalkers.

"Hurry, Sonya! They're recovering! Tell your girls to stay where they are, down there! If they move, I'll strike them as I stuck the guards. Tell them that!"

A lone hand! But I was winning.

We came to the front of the balcony stairway. The guards up there had vanished in fright. I mounted the steep stairs, with Sonya close under me.

Down on the terrace top, the guards had recovered, but they were too frightened to do anything but stare up at me.

I reached the balcony, moved to where there was no door behind me, where I could not be attacked unawares. And I drew Sonya to the balcony rail. Beneath us in the yellow moonlight the great throng of men, the girls, and the vanquished guards stood silently gazing up at me.

"Now, Sonya, I'll talk to them! Tell them I am Leonard Gray, the Earthman. Remind them that their king is dead; their prince is captured but a horrible unknown enemy that menaces us all!

Tell your girls that they shall have justice. Tell the men that we are going to rescue the prince! All of us united, not fighting one another.

"Tell them they have seen a little of my power. I want to use it for them, for you all, not against you! All of us united to rescue our prince. And until that is done — Leonard the Earthman is their ruler!"

XII

THE PRISONER IN THE CAVE

JIM HAD BEEN received by the dying king. For what seemed hours he sat with Ren in a castle room waiting to be admitted to the royal bedchamber. To Jim it was irksome. He was afraid the king would die, afraid something would go wrong, and we would all he held as prisoners again.

But he finally saw the king. Jim took the oath of allegiance, swore he would do what he could to rescue the prince.

They started back through the city streets. At this time I was with the girls on the Island of the Virgins. The Moon had just risen.

They were in the main lower street before our house. The Moon was still low at the horizon; its light was cut off by the houses. The street lamp shone full on the railed flower bed, but close to the buildings, under the pedestrian levels, the shadows were black. Jim suddenly became aware of peering green eyes, a black shape that leaped at him. Other shapes, with great wobbling heads.

A giant shape of human form had knocked Ren down. Another struck Jim, bore him with its weight to the pavement. His senses faded from a blow on the head, and blackness, smothered by clanging gongs in his ears as he lost consciousness.

For a moment, after an interval of what length he never knew, knowledge that he was still alive came to him. He seemed to remember that a giant manlike shape with a bullet head had leaped upon him. It had another head, huge, wobbling like a balloon. But the large head had fallen off it; the large head lay on the ground, with tiny arms supporting it.

The phantasmagoria of a dream. But Jim's head was clearing now, just a little. Something was holding him, and he could feel movement — a rhythmic jogging. He opened his eyes. A city street was passing. A great hairy arm was about his middle; he was being carried by something that walked; being held horizontal, his head, arms and legs dangling.

A giant, brown, hairy shoulder was over him; and above that, the great bulge of a head — a smooth, dead-white inflated membrane — a head that bounced and wobbled as the thing strode forward.

A brief consciousness, a vague, dreamlike impression, scarcely strong enough to make a memory, and Jim's senses again faded into a black voice of silence.

When Jim came fully to himself he was lying in a glow of yellow moonlight. Beneath him was a smooth, curving metal surface. His head ached horribly; a lump was upon it, and there was matted blood in his hair.

He was sore, bruised all over, but with returning strength he realized that he was not seriously injured.

He lay a moment, trying to remember what had happened, and the memory came, distorted and vague. Over him spread the canopy of stars, with a great yellow Moon rising. Was he on a boat? He was still no more than half-conscious. He murmured, "Ren! Ren!"

"Yes, Jim? Jim, is that you?"

Jim struggled up on one elbow. Ren was sitting hunched beside him. Ren — alive, seemingly uninjured.

They were in a boat, lying in its bottom, a small, narrow metal box, six feet wide perhaps, and perhaps five or six times as long. Its gunwale curved up two or three feet over Jim's head. They were lying in the narrowing of its bow.

Farther astern, in the yellow moonlight, were figures, brown, hairy bodies — men; or were they giant gorillas? They had small bullet-like heads, faces flat-nosed, with receding forehead and receding chin, and two small eyes that blazed green.

Jim very slowly sank back, but in a posture where he could see the length of the boat. The figures there were not animals; they were men of brute force and brute intelligence. Four of them, with powerful, hairy bodies, wide-shouldered, deep-chested, with short, thick legs and very long arms.

They were clothed in what seem trunks of animal skin, and a

skin fastened over the bulging chest to one shoulder. And each had a broad, tightly drawn belt at his waist.

To Jim came the memory of his capture. It was no fantasy, his memory of a hairy body, with a balloon-like, wobbling head. The four huge heads were here now, in a group near the center of the boat. Each was about four feet in diameter. A dead-white membrane, with bulging, distended veins on a forehead, over a grotesques flat face.

Heads, belonging to these four bodies? Jim realized it was not that. These were separate living entities, which had been riding astride the shoulders of the four.

Intelligent, reasoning beings — it seemed monstrous to call them men — beings which were nearly so distended that they sagged on their own weight.

As he regarded them, Jim became aware that to each of the great heads a shrunken semblance of body was attached. Two tiny arms, which came out directly from the sides of the head, and were now turned down, with hands pressing the boat to give balance.

From the wide, convex face, beneath what might have been a bloated chin, a shriveled body dangled: a trunk and legs some two feet long. They lay shriveled beneath the heads. Useless appendage! But all of these shrunken, dangling bodies were clothed with colored fabric, and upon the breast of one was an ornate metal ornament.

Jim whispered: "Ren?"

"Yes."

"What happened?"

"I don't know. Something struck me. Then somebody, something was carrying me. Men! I heard their voices. I tried to scream; a hand went over my mouth. I knew we were captured. I thought —"

"Hush! Not so loud! They're here . . . with us now."

"I know. They were talking a while ago. They — hear them now, Jim?"

Low, guttural voices sounded back there — the brute men. The brains, the balloon heads, were talking also, low, suave voices in a foreign tongue.

"Jim! Jim, one of these men here in the boat with us —" Ren's voice held a quiver of fear. "He's, Jim, I can receive his thoughts now . . . like Dolores did from a distance. It seemed, just a little while ago, that I was getting Len's thoughts. He was triumphant, exulting over something. But it was gone. Then I —"

"You get the thoughts of someone here in the boat?"

"Yes. I guess so. Someone . . . the thought came to me that he called himself Talon. I just now got it again. Talon. He's been studying thoughts from me. Putting them into my language. He's doing it now. It's very easy for him, studying my thoughts, our words . . . my words to you now. He can understand them."

"Hear us now?"

"Yes. Or hear the thoughts of our words. We can't escape! Can't do anything secretly! He's laughing at us. He —"

Jim saw one of the heads raise itself up on its hands. Its shriveled body hung limp, the body with the ornate cross on its breast. The arms bent, then straightened with a snap; the head bounded a foot or two in the air, landed again on its hands, and again leaped.

IT was hitching itself the length of the boat, its shriveled body trailing after it. One of the giant, hairy brutes of men moved aside to let it pass.

Jim whispered, "It's coming!"

A revulsion of horror swept him — a repugnance to have this great bloated head come near him. He strove to master the horror. This was a man. Strange of form, but a living, mortal being. A man — an enemy. Nothing supernatural, not gruesome, merely strange, an enemy with whom he had to cope.

Jim sat up abruptly. His shoulder touched Ren's. From down the boat the bloated head came hitchingly forward. A few feet from Jim and Ren it stopped, rested with a slight swaying upon the tiny body hunched under it.

Jim stared into a huge, convex face: round green eyes, holes, a circular rim of them, for nostrils, a wide mouth, thin-lipped. The mouth seemed almost a human feature; it was smiling. A soft, suave voice said,

"I . . . Talon." And corrected itself, "I mean . . . I am Talon."

It seemed to Jim in that instant that with those few spoken words the thing itself had removed most of the horror with which its outward aspect invested it.

A sense of relief swept over Jim. His tenseness relaxed. He said slowly: "What do you want of us, Talon?"

"Yes . . . Talon. " His arms had a hand, with a sheaf of broad, flat fingers. He pointed to the ornament hanging on the chest of his shrunken body. "Talon . . . leader of my people." He spoke haltingly, groping with the unfamiliar words, and carefully, as though to avoid error. "Called Talon. You . . . lie quiet and soon my words are more. I study. Lie quiet . . . until I speak again." He gestured. "Lie quiet, or —"

Another more vehement gesture. It embraced Jim and Ren. Jim understood the threat. The voice repeated very calmly, "You had better lie down . . . *now!*"

The eyes seemed leaping pools of green fire.

They sank back. With his elbows slightly raising him, Jim watched the head of Talon hitching itself to the stern of the boat.

The Moon had risen high above the horizon. From where Jim lay he could see its yellow, horn-shaped disk. That, and a narrow segment of the star-strewn sky, was all that showed above the gunwales of the boat. The stars rolled with a lazy swing; the boat was throbbing, propelled evidently, by some invisible engine, over a calm, rolling sea, and in the silence Jim could hear the water slipping past the boat's smooth sides.

He wondered how far from shore they were. If he and Ren, with a leap, could plunge overboard, a mad, foolhardy attempt, of course, but still he must see where they were, try and plan something.

"Ren?"

"Yes. What is it?"

"Move over a little. I'm going to get behind you and sit up, see where we are, how far from shore."

Jim cautiously raised his head. He half expected a command from the rear of the boat. But none came.

They were on a broad expanse of calm water. The Moon made a yellow shimmering path into which they were heading. Jim sank back. It would have been folly to have attempted an escape. For a long time he and Ren lay quiet. An hour, perhaps or more. The boat sped rapidly on.

Its invisible engine made a hiss, and a line of bubbles rose from its sides. Jim had noticed them when he sat up; the boat seemed traveling on a continuous, rising mass of bubbles. There was a queer acrid smell in the air from the gas of them.

Jim learned later from Talon the details of this boat. It was built of metal which, with its load, would barely float. Beneath the hull was a chamber through which the water circulated. A grid of wires was there; a current heated the wires, decomposed the water into its two component gases, hydrogen and oxygen.

The bubbles were buoyant. The rising flow of them lifted the boat, so that in truth it skimmed forward upon the gas bubbles beneath it. The generation of gases was controlled, so that the boat floated high or low at will. The engine was similar. The forcible ejection of gases from a tube extending under water from its stern propelled it forward. The tube was movable, like a rudder, to give direction.

An hour passed. Then the hairy brutemen who had been sitting quiet got to their feet, fumbled at the gunwales. An oval metal cover rolled from beneath the gunwales up like a canopy to enclose the boat overhead.

Jim had taken a last swift look outside, before the arched metal cover rolled and closed them in. The boat was now making for a sheer wall of cliff that lay directly ahead.

But in one place, for which they were steering, the cliff dropped sheer, unbroken into the water. Above the cliff, behind it, a jagged mountain range stood yellow in the moonlight, tumultuous, naked crags.

The cover closed overhead. A tiny green light winked on. Within the boat, lurid in the green glow, the four brutemen moved about with swift activity; the soft voice of Talon was directing them; his great head was raised on his hands as he followed their movements.

They bolted the metal over, adjusted other mechanisms which now came into use at the stern. A lessening of the flow of gas from beneath the hull; the water filled the chamber there. The rear power tube now pointed downward, to dip the bow. Other tubes, one on each side below the waterline, pointed upward, with powerfully ejected streams of gas.

The bow of the boat dipped; it sank beneath the surface. Jim had no idea then of the mechanisms, but he knew the boat was under water. One of the great heads was busily adjusting a mechanism to purify the air they were breathing. Another was seated at what seemed a mirror; gazing ahead through the water, steering the boat with his fingers on a row of buttons which governed the controls.

Another hour. Jim and Ren whispered occasionally. The boat was speeding uninterruptedly beneath the surface. At last Jim called,

"Talon?"

"Yes. What it is?" the head of Talon answered him.

"Come here. You can talk better now, can't you?"

Talon evidently was amused at the imperative tone. "Yes. I can talk better now."

He came hitching forward; his great face was broken by a grotesque grin. "What is it?"

"Who are you?" Jim demanded. "What do you want of us? Where are you taking us?"

Talon was willing to talk. He sat, his fingers toying with the metal ornament, his head resting against the side of the boat for support. He and his fellows were of a race which he called the Intellect. They came from a distant world in the sky, a dark planet, satellite of one of the remote suns up there.

Five thousand or more of them, adventurous Intelligences like himself, had built a great ship and come to this foreign world. They had landed in the mountains, a wild, desolate country. Their ship had been destroyed, irreparably broken in landing. They could not get back.

There were, he explained, in this distant world two distinct races of beings, those like himself, for countless ages bred to develop the intellect so that their bodies shriveled and dwindled from disuse, all their physical powers nearly gone. And another, quite opposite race, bred for physical strength and power, the brutemen, of slight mental capacity but powerful of body.

He gestured. "You see four of them? They do our bidding unquestioned. They supply the body for us; we are the mind."

"You ride on their shoulders," said Jim.

Talon's eyes gleamed. "We more than ride on them." He showed Jim where from beneath his head a ropelike sinew depended. "This we fasten upon a nerve-center on their backs. Their little brain is dulled, unconscious then of existence. Our brains take command.

"The body is ours, for a time! We can feel its physical power; our brain animates it. We are one being. One entity when that connection is made."

Ren spoke up softly, "Why did you go to that city where you captured us? Those people there haven't harmed you. But you captured their prince and princess."

The huge face grinned with a look of cunning. "We cannot get back to our world. We do not like these bleak mountains, these dark caves where we have been living. We must have a better land, and other people; we want to establish our own race. And there is little food, here in the mountains. We began wondering, searching. We brought this one boat with us from our own world." He described the workings of the boat and went on. "One day I came upon a man and that woman you call prince and princess. He says he is called Altho. They escaped from me, climbed to a cliff. But we caught them again finally."

He paused. Then he added slowly: "The princess is dead now. I did not want her to die . . . but the prince killed her."

It brought a shudder to Jim. He said, cautiously, "What are you going to do now? What do you want of us?"

"I was thinking that if you were important, like Prince Altho, to this other world, I might offer to release all of you, not kill you, if they would let us live among them in the city. But I have decided now not to bother with that. I think, if you annoy us too much, we shall kill you before we start."

"Start where?" Ren demanded. His voice was steady.

"Start upon our attack. We brought little with us from our world, a few devices and scientific supplies; but for all this time since we arrived we have been manufacturing. It is difficult with so few materials at hand. But we are nearly ready. When I return now, we will start our last preparations."

His voice rose to a sudden grim power, "We have prepared well for this conquest. It is a beautiful land down there; the women, so many of them like the princess, are very beautiful. The men, they are not like you two — they are already afraid of us. Some have seen us wandering near the cave entrance. They always run in terror."

His chuckle had a horrible gloating. "They will be easy to kill. A swift attack upon the city; we are almost ready for it now!"

The boat at last came to the surface; the cover rolled back; the stars gleamed overhead as before, but the yellow moon had crossed the sky and was falling to the horizon behind them. Jim saw that they had come to the surface of a very small lake.

He could see all around its shore, a circular lake of black, cold-looking water. It lay unrippled, smooth as polished black stone, unbroken except as the boat's gas bubbles rose, and by the V-shaped waves the boat left behind it.

Around the shore was a ring of mountains. Bleak, naked cliffs of rock came down sheer to the water; behind them the mountains rose in tumbled, serrated ranks, naked crags and spires, snow-capped with yellow snow where the moonlight struck them.

Here in the remote mountain fastness, Talon had established his stronghold. This was an isolated lake, which a subterranean boat had been plowing.

At Jim's elbow, Talon said, "These mountains seem to extend back endlessly. But I have another base already established on the Warm Sea, and from there I will make my attack. I have planned well."

Ahead of them, in one small place the mountains were broken. A narrow canyon-like valley was open to the water, with a fringe of black-sand beach. Cave mouths showed along the sloping valley sides. Lights moved. The mouths of the caves were outlined by a green-white glare from within.

The boat landed on the black beach. Brute figures crowded around it in the fading moonlight, sinister giant figures. Huge gruesome heads came bouncing forward over the sand. Voices sounded. Questions. The voice of Talon shouted commands.

Half a hundred of the brutemen lifted the boat bodily from the water, deposited it on the beach. Jim and Ren were carried up the valley, and into the green glow of a cave mouth. Ren seemed entranced.

Prince Altho faced Jim and Ren in the dimly lighted cave. Talon had left them. At the cave-mouth, barely beyond sight and hearing around an angle of its narrow entrance passage, two of the brutemen stood on guard. Altho's cave had been his home during most of his captivity. Jim saw it as a small room of glittering black rock, dimly lighted with pale green radiance from a ceiling tube from which green-glowing wires depended.

There was a bed of skins, crude stone furniture, a mere slab of rock for a table, upon which food now lay. Draped skins walled off a corner where the bed was placed.

Altho could not talk with Jim, but he very soon established that he was friendly. He was a man about Jim's height, this prince, but delicate, almost frail of build. A handsome square-jawed face, had the delicacy of royalty stamped upon it. A high, white forehead was topped with curly hair like pale gold.

He smiled and shook his head at Jim's voluble words. He shook hands with smiling puzzlement at Jim's insistence. He seemed to understand Ren's condition.

They sat, earnestly trying with gestures and words to make each other understand. Hours passed. Altho prepared some skins for beds, and gestured that they should sleep. Ren lay down, but Jim refused.

Another interval. A bruteman came with food. One of the heads, like Talon, came hitching itself in, looked around, spoke to Altho, and withdrew.

Jim ate some of the food. He had thought Ren was asleep, but when he questioned him, Ren sat up at once.

"Jim, what are we going to do?"

Jim was wondering that himself, and wondering also what fate Talon had in store for them. Abruptly Ren murmured,

"Awhile ago, Jim, I was sure I was getting someone's thoughts. Not Talon's; he's hiding them from me now. Someone like Len, or Dolores. Or perhaps it was Sonya."

Jim's heart leaped. Something was impending! He sat between them tensely; his hand touched Altho's arm; his eyes flashed at Altho with eager questioning.

Ren murmured, "I've got it now, Jim! It's Sonya! She says, *I am Sonya. We know you are with Altho. I am getting his thoughts, too!*"

A silence. Altho sat cross-legged on the stone floor, as Jim and Ren were sitting, with the stone slab of table before them; the green glow of light nearby threw shadows behind them. He looked up momentarily; his gaze rested on Jim and Ren with a new understanding, a new friendship.

Ren murmured, "She's telling Altho about us. She says, *Hold connection! I'm telling him . . . he's telling me —*"

Altho's lips were moving with his thoughts to Sonya. The girl, over all this distance, was translating from the universal language of thoughts for these two strangers at Jim's elbow.

Ren added, "Altho says to us in this thoughts, Talon had promised not to kill him; Talon now thinks he will be useful after our city of Kalima is conquered. But one of Talon's men — that head who was in here a while ago — he said they had decided we all three were to die. I'm asking Altho what he thinks we can do to escape."

Altho raised his head at the question; his eyes searched Ren's face. His lips moved.

"Jim! Jim, she says, *We are coming to try and rescue you! If you or Altho can direct us . . . we're coming . . . in the air now.*"

Altho was on his feet. He seemed to be warning Sonya back.

"No!" cried Ren. "Altho says no, they must not come! But they're coming! Sonya and . . . she doesn't say who's coming."

"What's that?"

Altho and Jim stiffened. From the entrance passage a figure had emerged, a giant, hairy bruteman. He stood with swaying, dangling arms, green eyes blazing in the pale green cave light; a leer on his small flat face, a black tongue like an animal's, licking his black lips with murderous anticipation!

XIII

CROWDED HOURS

"SONYA," I EXCLAIMED vehemently, "stay beside me! Don't leave me!"

How I cursed my inability to speak this language during those crowded hours following the king's death! At every turn, with every move I was handicapped, the force of my words lost since I had only a girl for mouthpiece.

Yet Sonya did well. The crowd in the garden had dispersed; Sonya had led the girls into cheering me. I had made a speech promising them justice in their cause, and sent them away, not to the Virgins' Island, but peacefully back to the homes they had left. They were glad to go; there was no government now to force them into a distasteful marriage.

The guards had come before me, at first with an indecision, a sullenness, but the old men counselors had swiftly abdicated.

"Tell them, Sonya, I want all their advice; whatever they think should be done, I will listen." I strode up and down the huge audience chamber of the castle, while the old men watched me with whispered, frightened words among themselves.

There was so much to do! I had made a speech to the men in the garden before they dispersed. Our prince must be rescued. They had a man of power and action leading them now.

My words, and perhaps my aspect as I stood up there in the moonlight, aroused them to enthusiasm. They were men. Courageous. Patriotic. They had never yet had a real leader. But they had one now.

It stirred me, as I had stirred them, when I heard them cheering.

I summoned the chief of the guards before me, a slim, straight young fellow with flashing eyes. When I demanded his allegiance — he and all his fellows' — he swung on his heel to the old men who ranged along the side of the room. They nodded timorously, and he turned back and bowed before me.

"Tell him, Sonya, that I want ten of his men always patrolling the castle grounds. And others, he can use his judgement as to numbers, patrolling the city. If there is any sign of disturbance, notify me at once. I want the people all to go to their homes and stay there."

There was so much that I did not know! "Sonya, are there any cities beside Kalima?"

"No," she said. "Only small villages. And there is the village on the Virgins' Island."

I nodded. "I want messengers sent out, to tell everyone of the change of government and a warning to beware of the Nameless Horror. It is abroad; it may appear anywhere. Have the people in the rural districts gather food and bar their homes, stay indoors. Sonya, who has been in charge of organizing the army?"

She named him, but it transpired that there had been nothing at all done, as yet, except a manufacturing of the weapons of war.

"Send him to me," I ordered. "And the leader of the scientists — he had been in charge of the manufacturing? I want to see him also."

Crowded hours! And I could not leave those girls on the Virgins' Island; a few of them had remained there with the old women and children. I ordered them all brought in; ordered such of them as could, to return to their former homes; the others were to be quartered in the castle.

Hours of swift, decisive commands followed. And there was no one in that busy castle, save possibly Sonya, who realized how I was groping. The government I had seized — *I* was the king now — a simple, primitive organization; but to me, so ignorant of its workings, it seemed complex indeed.

But I was learning. One by one, I had the leaders of its various departments brought before me, and from each, though they did not realize it, I learned a little more.

They were all very human. None were very hostile to the virgins; many now hoped they would be given their way.

All were afraid of the Nameless Horror, but all loved their

prince very dearly. It seemed that I would have no trouble with internal conditions.

Sonya soon realized it. Her voice carried a more commanding ring. Poor little Sonya! After hours of translating, issuing my commands, running my errands, she was on the verge of exhaustion. But, as in us all, the spirit of battle was upon her. An enemy was at our doors, and soon everyone realized that every command I issued was to make us stronger to resist that enemy.

It had been well over an hour after my abrupt seizure of the castle, before I even thought of Alice and Dolores. They were unharmed. Sonya had kept them away from the castle steps; for half an hour they had been in the room with me, watching and listening with wide eyes and solemn faces, a half hour before I saw them. They did not question, but ran to Sonya and me to be of such help as they could.

Once Alice insisted, "You must rest, Leonard. You can't keep this up, you and Sonya." I had never before seen the light of love for me in her eyes, but I saw it then!

I had sent the girls into a castle room to sleep. At last I was alone with food, and a hot stimulating drink, like coffee, before me. I was seated at a table, in the king's huge chair. *I* was the king. Alone here in my audience room. Through the windows, the falling Moon threw a yellow glow. The time of sleep was nearly over. The city was awakening; I could hear its voice awakening to the round of daily activity.

My city now! But the thought brought no exultation. This new day would be dark like the other. If the Nameless Horror were abroad in the city — Had I not better form an armed street patrol? And keep the people indoors? I needed more messengers.

The young men from the outlying districts must be ordered in to enroll with my recruiting staff. Suppose the people outside of Kalima revolted against me? Would I have to go out and overawe them with the Frazier beam?

Maxite, the scientist, was coming back to talk with me presently. I thanked God that he at least had learned from Ren my language. So much to do, and I was so tired!

My head fell to my hands on the table. Alone there at last in the great, silent room, I fell asleep.

"Why —"

* * *

"YOU'VE BEEN ASLEEP, highness. I did not want to awaken you."

Maxite sat across the table from me. I aroused myself, rubbing my eyes, embarrassed at my undignified position. Maxite had evidently been sitting there a long time, waiting for me to have my sleep out. The moonlight was gone. The windows were black rectangles, the stars hidden by dark-gray cloud masses. But the city was awake, its new day now fully advanced.

Maxite smiled. He was a small, gray-haired man of middle age, black-robed, with gray ruching at his throat and wrists, and with a yellow ball ornament dangling from a chain at his neck. He said,

"Others, too, are waiting to have your orders, highness. But we knew you needed rest."

At the farther door of the large apartment a group of men and a few girls were standing. One by one, I saw them. My chief of the guards reported that the city seemed normal; the Nameless Horror had not appeared. A messenger from the rural districts along the Warm Sea said the people were frightened.

They were obeying my orders to stay indoors; but the young men were demanding that I let them come at once to Kalima, to get from me weapons with which to defend their families.

Three girls presented themselves, with a petition that the girls be allowed to join the army. Five hundred names were on it. A fat, affluent-looking individual, a wealthy landowner he told me, came to present his claim to immediate marriage to a girl who was now returned from the Virgins' Island. I sent him brusquely away.

There was some confusion over the return of the refugees from the island. Some of the infants could not be returned to their homes; the mothers were afraid to have them. Some of the virgins lived in the rural sections; they wanted their parents brought into the city for greater safety. And some of the old women had not been welcomed home, and had been brought to the castle.

I did my best to straighten it out. Enlistment in my army had already begun. I interviewed three trainers of the military animals, for use on land, in the water, and in the air. The animals were ready. The mechanical equipment was very nearly complete.

I sent word to the rural districts for all young men to come in and present themselves to my recruiting officers. And any family that wished, could come also. I issued a proclamation to the city, that all homes be prepared here in Kalima to care for at least one family of refugees, at government expense if necessary.

Expense! My national treasurer was already in despair. I knew almost nothing of my nation's finances, but I did not admit it. I would learn, devise some methods of raising money. Already a dozen ways were springing to my mind. That fat, middle-aged landowner, for instance, he and others like him would not be so rich when I got my government properly operating.

Maxite and I were alone again. "Come," I said. "I'm ready."

We had planned that he would show me through the arsenal. I wanted first to see the small hand weapons. Maxite had told me that we had a room with a thousand or more electronic needle pipes, a simple hand device which generations ago had been used for hunting birds.

The army would be equipped with it, Maxite planned. I thought, too, if it were sufficiently simple, I would send it into the rural districts, so that each home might be armed for defense.

"I want also," said Maxite, "to show you our aerial image-finders."

These, which he had already described, I needed at once. Our enemy — I still could only call it the Nameless Horror — probably had a base near Kalima. Prince Altho perhaps was in captivity there; Jim and Ren, if they were alive, might be there also. This aerial device might enable me to locate the enemy base.

Maxite and I were descending into the lower floors of the castle. We passed rooms where the refugees were huddled. Girls had been organized to care for them. On another, still lower floor, I saw my guard pacing back and forth through dim stone corridors. We were now below the terrace level, but higher than the level of the back street.

We descended other floors, came to a narrow dark corridor. This, Maxite told me, was at the street level of the back castle wall. I remembered walking along that curving street, at the base of the wall, remembered a small door there.

"It's here," said Maxite.

We stood in a dim blue radiance at the intersection of two

corridors. Ahead lay a floor-opening, where down a flight of curving stone steps was the entrance to the first of the subterranean arsenal rooms. To the right, a branching passageway led to the small street gateway.

"A guard is there," said Maxite, "armed with a fire-flash for close-range work. He could kill anyone who came near him. Oh Grett!"

He called the guard but there was no answer. His soft voice echoed between the narrow passage walls. We hastened to the gate door. The guard was not there! But in the darkness we heard a sound. Maxite's hand-wire in its blue tube flung a faint beam around us. On the stone flagging a figure lay twisting. We had heard the scrape of movement. It was the guard, lying there bound and gagged!

XIV

FUGITIVES IN THE STARLIGHT

I HAD SENT Alice, Sonya and Dolores into one of the castle bedrooms. They were all tired and overwrought with the excitement through which they had passed. A dream awakened Sonya, after how long an interval she did not know — several hours undoubtedly. She dreamed she had been talking with Prince Altho: he was in a cave; Jim and Ren were with him.

For a long time Sonya lay pondering. Then she awakened the other two girls.

"Listen, I want to go and try and rescue Altho."

She told them her plan. They could take a small flying platform, with a few birds. Once away from the city, the distraction of thought-waves of all its people, she would be able to communicate with Altho or with Ren. Communicate with them, find them — rescue them!

A mad, impossible adventure, perhaps, but to the girls it looked feasible.

"Oh, Alice, oh, Dolores, shall we try it? Leonard will be many days getting his army together. That is too dangerous, to wait so long."

Dolores turned to her with shining, tearful eyes. "If I could only get to Jim, help him to safety."

Sonya had other plans. She could get weapons, a small weapon, the electronic needle pipe. She knew where they were kept, and how to use them.

"I heard Ren discussing it one day with Maxite the scientist. And there are image-finders stored in the same room. I think I know how to use them."

The girls decided to try it. They slipped unobserved from the room. Sonya found them long, hooded black cloaks. In the darkness, mingled with the confusion of arriving refugees, they got out of the castle without being recognized.

"Where are we going?" Dolores whispered. They were all three tense with excitement. Sonya had turned toward the rear of the castle, into the dimly lighted street along the base of the wall.

"A gate-door here," she whispered. "It is guarded by Grett. Quiet! Stand close beside me, but do not speak. But be ready to do what I say. Soon we will have the weapons."

In the castle bedroom, before leaving, Sonya had torn a garment into long, narrow strips, a staunch, tough fabric. She handed the strips now to Alice. At the small door in the wall, they paused.

"Keep behind me," Sonya whispered. "Over there in the shadow. But be ready."

The street along here was dark; it was a street little used and at the moment it was empty. Sonya knocked boldly on the door.

"Grett! Oh, Grett!"

In her own language from within came a muffled question. "Who is there?"

"It's Sonya."

"Yes?"

"Open the door."

"No. I must not."

"It's only Sonya. Don't you know my voice?"

"Yes. What do you want?"

"I've news from Ren. He is . . . Oh, Grett, you must let me show you."

There was the sound of dropping metal bars. The door opened cautiously a trifle.

Sonya put her hand casually on the door. "It's only Sonya, Grett. See here what I have."

She tugged at the door. The guard was revealed, standing with the leveled metal pipe in his hand. Sonya touched the weapon. "Turn it away Grett. It . . . frightens me!"

There was a low cry, a scuffle. Sonya had snatched the pipe. She leaped backward, swung it level.

"Don't move, Grett! Don't make a sound! If you do I . . . I'll kill you!"

"Sonya!"

"I'm desperate! Can't you see it? Get back in there!" She called softly, "Alice! Dolores! Here! Come inside, quickly."

She had backed the frightened, surprised young man into the corridor, with leveled weapon and crisp menacing words. In the glow of the passageway's single light, she held the weapon while Alice and Dolores bound the man's legs and arms with the strips of fabric. Sonya gagged him, and they rolled him along the floor to the wall and left him.

Alice was grim and pale, frightened at what they had done. Dolores was trembling. "We haven't hurt him, have we?"

Sonya bent down, loosened the gag a trifle. "No, he's all right. Lie quiet, Grett. And when they find you, tell them you're not to blame. Sonya tricked you. We may be back by then, anyway, and I'll take the blame."

The girls hurried down the corridor, down the stone steps into the arsenal room. Sonya had been here once before with her uncle. The place was dark, but Sonya found a hand-wire and Alice carried it above her head. Its light glowed dimly blue, in a big room of fearsome shadows. Overhead they could hear the faint tramp of a guard. Every moment they expected to be discovered.

Sonya seized one of the electronic needle pipes, and the range apparatus with which to operate it. And a large metal cylinder in which was packed a group of image-finders and their aerial controls. At the gate-door they switched off the corridor light. Sonya murmured, "Good-bye, Grett!"

They closed the gate-door after them. From the outside it appeared barred. With the cloaks shrouding them they hurried to Sonya's house.

In a moment they had six birds harnessed to a small platform, and were in the air.

Within the cave, Altho, Jim and Ren faced the giant murderous intruder. The bruteman stood licking his lips, an imbecile leer on his face.

There was a brief silence.

Altho spoke soft, soothing words to the hairy giant, and then ripped out a sharp command. It went unheeded. The bruteman's dangling hand came up to his belt. But never reached it.

Jim screamed an exclamation to Ren, and leaped. His body struck the bruteman full, a solid impact which would have flung Jim back, but the giant's huge arm went around him, lifted him like a child. As he went up, he flung his arms around the thick, hairy neck and clung.

His feet were high in the air as the bruteman straightened with a savage, surprised cry. He tried to shake Jim off, but Jim clung with one arm, with the other hand he gouged at the giant's face.

Altho had leaped. The giant kept his feet, swaying, kicking; he stopped, and with an upflung arm, dashed Jim's body away. But Jim was back at him again, he and Altho, now, clinging, kicking, gouging.

And then Ren. The harassed giant, fighting with scarce the intelligence of a man, staggered across the cave with Altho and Jim clawing at him. Their bodies struck Ren, and scrambling in the dark, he caught a great hairy leg and wound himself around it.

In the pale-green glow of the cave, the giant bruteman surged about. He tripped, went down, with the three men pounding on top of him.

Jim shouted, "We've got him!"

But the giant was up, shaking them off, first one, then another, tearing them loose, flinging them back. But always they returned to claw at him. They fought silently, grimly, but the giant roared.

Harassed, frightened, Altho had torn his belt away and flung it aside. The giant stood panting, looking around to see where it had gone. Altho was gripping his thick middle firmly with both hands; Ren was wound about his legs.

Jim had been flung away again. He was picking himself up, but he stopped. He had seen a jagged, metallic projection of the cave-wall. It seemed loose. Jim tugged at it. The swaying bodies surged past him. He tugged, worked it loose. It came free; in his hand he held a heavy, jagged chunk of black metal.

"Ren! Work him over this way! Over here . . . here!"

Jim leaped to the slab of table for greater height. The giant's back was to it. Jim could not talk to Altho, and Altho could not see him. But he could hear Jim's reiterated call.

The bruteman tried to turn toward the insistent voice, but Altho now understood and distracted his attention. And Ren at his legs, was pushing him backward. A step; then another.

They came within reach of the table. Jim leaped into the air. He struck the giant's back; his hand went up, and the heavy chunk of metal caught the bruteman full on the back of the skull.

He toppled, fell writhing, jerking a moment, then lay still.

They disentangled themselves from him, and stood up. They were all three bruised and winded. There was a jagged cut on Jim's forehead; he dashed the blood from his eyes.

"Let's get out of here! Now's the time! Now, or never!"

Altho's pale face smiled at him questioningly.

Jim gestured. "Out . . . get out of here!" He added, "The belt. What'd you do with the belt?"

The giant's weapons. Altho could not understand the words, but Jim saw the belt. He leaped over the huge, motionless body. Outside the cave an uproar sounded.

Altho called a warning; he was gesturing vehemently at Jim to come. Jim seized a small metal object at random from the giant's belt, an egg-shaped thing of white metal: a muzzle-projection, a handle and a trigger.

Lights were moving nearby in the darkness with a confusion of voices. The second of the giant guards at Altho's cave had run away in fear. He was shouting, gathering others over the rocks; calling commands. The brute-bodies were running to them, each to his master. The heads were mounting. . . .

Jim turned to the right, up the valley. They were momentarily in darkness, open metallic ground up a rocky slope, stars overhead, lights and confusion behind them.

They ran. Jim had handed the giant's weapon to Altho, thinking he would know better how to use it. They ran swiftly. A tiny light to one side picked them out, then it vanished. Jim pulled them sidewise to change their course. Ren stumbled over the rocks as they ran, but they kept him on his feet.

Jim panted, "A cliff . . . over there! We can climb it . . . or hide."

Altho glanced back. The lights were rushing on up the valley. The fugitives were running between jagged, tumbled boulders; Jim thought they had eluded the pursuit. But suddenly ahead of them, a head rose on its hands from behind a crag.

Jim jumped for it. He struck it. His fist struck the great face between its green blazing eyes. The face smashed, cracked like the shell of an egg. Noisome! His fisk sank into a soft pulpy mass. He jerked it free. The head rolled backward, the arms waving.

"Come on," Jim shouted. He wiped his fist and arm on his jacket: noisome, horrible!

"We're on the ledge, Ren . . . can't climb out of the valley. It's too steep."

"Are they following us?"

"No. I can see lights going up the valley. Altho seems to want to lie here, not try to climb higher. If only I could talk to him."

"I'm trying to get Sonya's thoughts, Jim."

They lay on a dark ledge; a fifty-foot drop was before them, a sheer perpendicular wall. They had climbed beside it, where the ground was broken. Over the ledge, some ten feet above it, was another, broader space with what seemed a cave-mouth behind it. The crags were dim in the starlight; black gullies, ravines were everywhere. Below them spread the valley floor. Lights which marked the pursuit had gone past.

For a time the three fugitives lay quiet. Jim's mind went back to the cave from which they had escaped. Two of the brutemen had been on guard.

These brutemen were hardly more than animals, like tigers with a lust for human blood. One had murderously entered the cave; the other, listening, had become frightened and decamped, giving the alarm.

Jim whispered impatiently, "Ren, can't you get any thoughts from Sonya?"

"No. I'm trying. I feel . . . I feel that Altho is getting them."

It seemed so. Altho was lying with his head down on his hands. Once he uttered a suppressed exclamation, and then he was murmuring as though to himself.

"You're right. He's getting them," Jim muttered. "Try again, Ren!"

Abruptly Ren exclaimed, "They're coming! Sonya, with Dolores and Alice."

"Do they know where we are?"

"They're trying to find us. Sonya says they haven't seen any lights yet to mark our valley. Altho has been trying to direct them."

"Well, for a while we're safe. They —"

Jim never finished. From down the valley, by the cave-lights of Talon's encampment, a ball of fire mounted slowly upward, a tiny, blazing white ball. It rose in a slow arc, and suddenly burst with a blinding white glare.

They valley, the crags, the ledge upon which the fugitives lay were all momentarily brilliantly illuminated. Jim saw that beneath them in the valley a hundred of the mounted heads were gazing upward. And he knew, too, that they had been seen upon the ledge.

A shout arose; a rush of the figures to climb. But a voice, Talon' s voice, seemed commanding them to stop. Farther down the valley, brutemen were dragging forward a heavy piece of equipment, a huge gun-muzzle on wheels, the muzzle pointed vertically upward.

Jim leaped to his feet. "We've got to get higher! Try to get to that cave overhead."

But Altho pulled him back. Altho still held the weapon Jim had taken from the giant. He gestured with it. Jim sank back.

There was something going on down there in the valley. Jim wondered if the weapon Altho had was of any use at this distance. Altho seemed absorbed in thought communication. Suddenly from over the cliff-tops across the valley, a small pink ball of light came sailing, floating over the valley in a huge segment of circle, a thousand feet in the air.

A glowing pink ball; a concentrated radiance seeming to whirl upon its axis, with tiny crescent streamers of light as it whirled. It sailed in a curve above the valley, growing dimmer, as though burning itself out, until in a moment it vanished.

Jim stared. But Altho knew what it was. He leaped to his feet.

XV

THE RESCUE

THE SMALL FLYING platform, with the girls prone upon its fur covering, sailed up from Sonya's home and over the city. The stars were obscured by gathering black clouds, a threatening storm, but it did not break. Sonya headed the birds for the Virgins' Island.

They pressed a thousand feet above it where a barge drawn by swimming sea animals below was bringing the women and children back to Kalima. Sonya had only the general direction of where she wanted to go, the length of the Warm Sea toward the distant mountains and caves. The Nameless Horror had been seen always in that direction.

The girls lay silent. Sonya was in constant, though sometimes vague communication with Altho. She knew the captives were in a cave; then she got the thoughts clearer, and got Ren's thoughts also. But suddenly all the thoughts were broken.

The threatening storm passed. The Moon was below the horizon. But the stars came out clear and bright. The girls were calmer now, grim with purpose. Sonya began connecting their scientific apparatus, explaining it as well as she could.

The electronic needle pipe was a foot-long metallic pipe with a diameter the size of a small human finger. It had a large, round metallic base, to be operated by two hands.

It projected a very small stream of electrons, which carried with them a tiny, sharp-pointed fragment of metal, like a needle. The needle flew with nearly the speed of light, expanding, But when it struck it solidified.

There was a range finder for aiming, and a device for curving the electronic stream, so that the beam could be sent to almost any degree of curvature. In her hear, though she did not confess it even to herself, Sonya was dubious of her ability to use the weapon.

She knew she could not aim it with any degree of skill. And she did not know its range. This needle pipe was a very small size projector, with a range, she thought, effective only a few hundred feet.

The girls were now beyond the Warm Sea, flying over a broken, mountainous country, black and desolate looking in the starlight. Altho's thoughts were with Sonya again. They had never been as clear as this before. A fight, an escape, a dark ledge with a valley below it. There were lights in the valley.

But where, in all this dark, mountainous waste, was that valley? Sonya believed she was flying toward it. She had several times in the last hour altered the direction of the flight. Altho's thoughts, a dim feeling of his approaching nearness, seemed to guide her.

It was very vague, an intuition more than a thought. Altho himself did not know where he was, but the bond of love between these two was very strong. Each could feel the other's approaching presence. He had tried to warn her away, but when she persisted, he did his best to guide her.

Sonya murmured, "Now he says, *Lights in the valley — you will see the lights.*"

But every desolate valley sweeping beneath them was pale and wan in the starlight. Then Sonya prepared an image-finder. She connected the batteries, the projector, and the grid of glowing wires.

Alice and Dolores held the grid between them. Sonya fired the small projectile. It sailed off, a whirling pink ball. It was in reality a small, flat disk with a lens-like eye and a whirling pink, glowing armature on top.

Over a radius of several miles Sonya's *raytron* apparatus could direct its flight, and back over the invisible connecting ray came an image of all that the lens eye saw.

The pink ball of light sailed ahead and soon was lost to view. The grid of wires which Alice and Dolores held glowed pink; then suddenly glared white. A glare of white showed ahead of them in the sky. It was the light flare Talon had sent up to locate the fugitives.

The flare went dark. The grid was pink again. Upon it, etched in black, was a moving scene: mountains, crags, valleys, moving in slow panorama, valleys all pale and empty in the starlight. Then one showed dim, moving lights!

Alice cried, "Sonya . . . lights! We see them now!"

Sonya's apparatus marked the position of the pink ball. She turned the birds slightly, to fly after it.

The platform was almost over the valley. Sonya sent out another pink disk. The girls bent over the grid, staring at the tiny movement image; a dim, starlit valley. At the bottom of it, a group of busy figures and a giant projector muzzle pointing vertically upward.

The girls watched the grid breathlessly. Its image, moving with constantly changing viewpoint, was clearly etched, but dim and very small: a cliff ledge with three figures upon it. From the ledge suddenly a small red ring of fire leaped out. It sped downward, struck a rock, and vanished in a puff.

It was Altho firing the weapon Jim had taken from the giant; in a moment the still distant girls heard a report, like a tiny clap of thunder, the sound of the red ring striking the rock. Down in the valley the giant muzzle of the vertical projector began issuing a stream of green light.

It mounted a hundred feet, sprayed out like a fountain column of water. From the ground, huge black figured tossed a balloon head into the column of light. The head rose, surged upward, until at the top it hung in the light spray, balancing itself like a ball held at the top of a jet of water.

It was all very swift, a moment or two while the girls stared at the glowing grid. The head was nearly level with the ledge. In the green light Altho's figure showed plainly; he was standing at the ledge, firing his red rings of flame.

But they were futile now. They floated slowly, and from below, some hidden marksman was catching each of them with an upflung pencil point of black light, a narrow beam, so dead black that it showed clearly in the night. It caught the red fire rings; its rays exploded them harmlessly in the air.

The grid went dark; the second lens disk had burned out. But the platform itself now swept over the valley. The reality of the image scene was spread beneath the girls. Sonya saw the ledge was large enough to land upon; she guided the birds toward it.

She raised the electronic needle projector, fired it with a futile aim and then cast it away. There was no time for her to attempt to use it further. Her birds were swooping for the ledge, and they needed her guidance. A moment, and they would be there.

But too late! The head in the fountain of green light held something in his hands. A hum rose over the valley. Altho, standing on the ledge, suddenly flung up his arms. His weapon fell from him. He toppled, seemed trying to draw himself backward. But could not.

And then, forward from the ledge his struggling figure floated into the air. On the ledge, Ren and Jim were frantically clinging to avoid being drawn after him. The hum rose to a shrill whine.

In what seemed a whirlpool of air, or the levitation of an invisible magnetic stream, Altho was drawn to the head on the supporting green light beam. The green light slowly diminished.

The head, with arms holding Altho's unconscious body, was lowered to the ground. A voice down there shouted hurried commands. The lights all went out sharply. In the starlight, Altho's body was surrounded by dark surging figures, and dragged away.

The platform swooped to the ledge, landed with a thump.

"Jim! Jim! Are you all right?" It was Dolores's anxious voice. But Sonya was cold, shuddering. All her hopes had vanished. She knew that they could not go down into the dark valley, with all those armed figures entrenched in the caves. Altho was lost to her.

Jim and Ren rushed to the platform. There was a moment of confused greeting. Jim never knew how it quite happened, but from the other ledge, ten feet above them, a head like Talon suddenly leaped down. It flashed to Jim that the head must all this time have been laboriously climbing in the darkness. Or perhaps had followed some underground passage to the cave up there.

Dolores was standing slightly apart from the others. The head seized her. On the upper ledge a giant bruteman was leaning down; the head tried to lift Dolores to where the dangling arms of the bruteman could reach her, arms which would have pulled her and the head both up to the upper ledge.

It happened so quickly, it was so utterly unexpected, that Jim and the other two girls were for an instant stricken with surprise.

Dolores screamed. It was the first that they knew of her peril. She called, "Jim! Jim!"

But Ren was closer. He leaped before Jim, leaped in the dark for the girl's terrified voice. He struck the head with his shoulder. His groping arms tore Dolores away.

There was a spurt of flame from some weapon the head was carrying. It caught Ren in the chest, drilled him. He fell backward, lay motionless. Btu he had saved Dolores from her captor. Jim and Alice had reached her.

The bruteman leaned swiftly down. The head held up one of its small arms. The bruteman drew his master to the upper ledge, with a jerk as though he were raising a large, light ball. In the valley they were trying to raise another beam of the green light.

Jim was carrying Dolores; he threw her to the platform and dragged Ren's inert body aboard, with Alice grimly helping him. Sonya screamed at the birds.

From above, the head was sending down tiny spurts of flame. They struck the fur coverings with the acrid smell of burning hair. Jim flung the girls behind him; every moment he expected that the flame jets would strike him.

It was only an instant, then the platform lifted, sailed away. The ledge dropped beneath it. The dark, seemingly deserted valley dropped and merged into the tumbled mountain waste.

The platform struggled on, sailing low. It was at the Virgins' Island now. The Moon was rising again with its flood of yellow radiance. Ahead, toward Kalima, they saw a blob in the sky.

It was the large flying platform I had hastily equipped and armed, coming out over the city to seek them.

But Ren was dead.

XVI

DEPARTURE FOR BATTLE

WE WERE READY at last for our attack upon Talon's forces. The night had passed, and another long day, and night had come again. Jim's return, with what he had to tell us about Talon, was of immeasurable help to me. I knew now what I was facing.

It was tremendously helpful also in arousing public enthusiasm for the war. The Nameless Horror was nameless no longer. The people recognized that a savage enemy was at their threshold, men who would have to be fought and conquered.

I did not want a large fighting force, but I wanted it well armed and trained, armed for defense also against what I could guess Talon's weapons might be. Jim had seen something of them.

I sent out scouting platforms with the aerial image-finders. But they brought me little information, for presently Talon realized what the pink balls of radiance in the sky meant. He began destroying them with his black flash beam.

This was to be a war of weapons, rather than fighting men. With Maxite, I labored to prepare a defense against Talon's black flash, and the fire rings which Altho had used. Evidently Talon was armed chiefly with weapons of electronic basis. I hoped so, for we could insulate against them fairly efficiently.

The day had just turned to night when news came that Talon's forces had left the mountains and now were encamped at the end of the Warm Sea. It was what I had hoped he would do. I had no intention of allowing him to attack Kalima, but I did not want to go up into the mountains after him. He was evidently ready now, but so was I.

It was a busy time, those last hours. Kalima was jammed with refugees. All along the shores of the Warm Sea the rural districts were deserted. I mobilized my men and girls on the castle grounds, and on the estuary there. The girls had had their way; they were an important unit of my forces. I could not refuse them, for they speedily demonstrated that in the air they were far superior to the men.

With Sonya and Maxite, I stood on the Castle terrace watching the last details of our departure. The night was clear, save for a low bank of clouds hanging over the sea, with the horn-shaped yellow Moon rising above it.

The castle grounds were crowded with my eight hundred fighting men, two hundred girls, the land animals, birds and platforms. On the water were the boats, with sea animals to draw them. I had some four hundred men in this division — a total of about fourteen hundred.

A busy scene of moving lights, voices, commands, the fluttering of the excited birds; behind us, on every housetop, in every window and point of vantage in the city, a throng of spectators watched.

The last preparation held a myriad details.

"Maxite," I said, "the platform with the Frazier beam — have them hold it until last. Then I'll come down."

Maxite's orders went out over the aerial he carried on his shoulder. I could hear the echo of his voice down there in the garden. I swung the grid on my chest to catch the rays from an image-finder erected on the waterfront. Alice and Dolores were down there. I had not wanted them in this fighting, but they insisted, and I had put them in the division of boats.

"All ready, Alice?"

She glanced up at the image-finder; it stood on a post at the shorefront. On my grid was the image of her figure standing there, with her insulated suit like a black cone around her, and her helmet in her hand. "All ready, Leonard." Her smile was grim, excited, tense, but I could see no fear in it.

"Be careful, Alice. Keep Dolores with you . . . and obey orders."

"Yes." She turned away.

Sonya, standing beside me, laid her hand on my arm. "We're going to win, Leonard. And Altho —" She gestured. "I seem always to be getting his thoughts, Leonard. Again . . . just now."

We knew that Altho was still alive, that Talon was going to keep Altho with him. Sonya very often had fragmentary communication. She had seemed to be getting it a few hours ago, and now, suddenly, we realized what evidently Altho had been trying to tell her. A messenger rushed up. He had come from one of our scout platforms.

Talon's forces had started for Kalima. The brutemen with the heads mounted upon them were dragging heavy apparatus along the shore road. And there were rafts on the sea drawn by swimming brutemen. The rafts were already half way to the Virgins' Island!

There was no time to be lost. Maxite's aerial sent his voice to the seventy men and twenty girls who were equipped to receive it. Each of them urged his squad to greater haste.

The individual girl flyers rose first. One by one, each mounted upon a giant bird, they rose from the castle grounds, and began circling in the air. These girls were not protected against Talon's electric rays.

It was my plan to keep them very high in the air, beyond what we estimated was the effective range of Talon's black flash. They were armed only with small explosive bombs, but were expert at dropping them upon a mark.

A hundred and fifty of these mounted girls gathered now in a hovering group, then in wedge-shape, flew in a wide, slow circle. The birds were well-trained, capable of flying swiftly to great heights. And the most agile of the young girls; Sonya had selected them carefully.

This unit was the swiftest, most mobile of my forces. Sonya was to lead it. She was presently ready, bringing up her great gray bird, with its rug saddle upon which she would recline on its back between its great spreading wings.

She was dressed, as were all the girls in the air squadron, in a single dark flowing garment from shoulder to knee, with her hair bound tightly in braids around her head. The small metallic bombs were in a belt at her waist, bombs fitted with a chemical most explosive.

She offered her hand in my own fashion.

"Good-bye," I said. "And remember, Sonya, keep well up, and listen to my signals. Do not attack until I order it."

She leaped upon her mount. It rose over me with dangling legs; the rush of air from its wings was on my face. In a moment I saw her up there, taking her place just below the girl at the point of the wedge.

From the garden, the first of the flying platforms rose. There were three of this size, each with twenty men and some ten girls. Forty birds were harnessed to each platform: birds in tandem along each side, and two long strings in front. Four girls were to drive them; the other girls had bombs, and the men had the smaller range electronic needle-pipes.

These platforms were fairly swift. They were insulated underneath, with the shaggy black fabric of woven wire through which the insulating current circulated. And they had side shields which could be raised; and dangling, insulating curtains beneath some of the birds.

I stood watching the three platforms as they rose majestically, joined the mounted girls, and circled with them over the city.

The land forces were starting. Jim was leading this division: eight hundred men, most of them mounted individually upon the giant *lops* — a four-footed animal, more like a giant cat than anything I can name; handsome beasts, larger than an Earth-horse, with great claws, a mass of shaggy red hair, and a tail like a plume of fur.

Each with a rider, they padded through the village streets. Some were harnessed to our larger projectors, and our wind device, which I planned to have Jim establish down the shore opposite the Virgins' Island. With it, Jim could lash the narrow channel waters to a fury.

The small land force passed into the city and vanished. From the distant housetops, I could see the waving crowd to mark its progress. I turned away. The boats on the river had started, a fleet of ten long, narrow, metallic boats, with insulated sides and shields, boats drawn by seal-like mammals, agile, swift and intelligent.

There were some forty men and a few girls on each of the boats. A large long-range needle projector was mounted in the bow, behind the black screen.

It could throw an electrified, imponderable blade of metal over a curved path, with almost the speed of light for an effective distance of over a mile. And these boats had light-flares, wind projectors, and horizontal bomb projectors.

They sped down the estuary, with the mammals leaping like

dolphins in the water ahead of them; then they stopped, circled, came back, and waited in a line in midstream. From the city a great shout of enthusiasm went up at sight of them. On one of them were Alice and Dolores.

Our three other flying platforms were long strings of birds, our longest-range rising, heavier, smaller platforms, each with weapons — a giant projector on each of them, with a few men to handle it.

Maxite said, "We're ready for you, Leonard." He had dropped, for the first time, my royal title. We stood, two friends, parting with a handclasp. His face was very solemn. I think he, too, was thinking of the homecoming. "I'll follow you with the finders, Leonard. Keep voice connection if you can. Perhaps . . . I will see what you might overlook, and I can advise you."

I nodded. A simple handclasp. He turned away, to watch our fate from his room beneath the castle.

My platform with the giant Frazier thought-beam we had constructed, was ready. I was to operate it alone. I had learned to fly its six birds. I clasped my black, cone-shaped robe about me. My black helmet dangled like a hood behind my shoulders.

I ran down the castle stairway. From the city a roar of enthusiasm went up. I turned and waved a hand.

Departure for battle! The people expected a martial gesture, and I gave it to them. But within me was a shudder.

I leaped on the black platform. It was no more that six feet wide and twice as long, crowded with the projector, the batteries and intensifiers, and much more scientific apparatus.

I gripped the reins, shouted to the six birds whom I had trained to know my voice and respond to my commands.

My platform rose over the castle grounds. Around me, the girls and the other platforms circled. Down in the estuary the ten black boats were starting in a double line. Out beyond the city, on the road toward the sea, a thin black line showed in the yellow moon-glow — Jim's land division. The city beneath me was a frantic, waving mass of humanity.

I shouted through my aerial. The girls and the platforms broke their circle and started forward. With my platform leading them, we swept in a great arc over the city, and away into the moonlit sky.

XVII

THE BATTLE

THE WARM SEA was a body of water some one hundred miles long by ten miles wide at most places. It lay in a bowl-like depression of rolling country. Bays and caves indented its shores in some places; in others cliffs came sheer to the water.

Kalima lay at what I might term it southern end. The sea broadened here into a sheet of water nearly twenty miles wide, which I had learned to call Kalima Bay. To the north it narrowed. The Virgins' Island divided it, with a narrow channel on each side, beyond which it opened again.

To the left along the west side of the sea, the road from Kalima wound northward. The west channel of the Virgins' Island was very narrow — two thousand feet at the utmost — but it was very deep, with a sandy strip of beach on the mainland, a bluff of fifty feet, with the road on top. It was along the west side that Talon's land forces were coming. And on the same road from Kalima Jim's force was marching to oppose them.

Our water division of ten boats headed into the center of Kalima Bay, and there I halted them. They lay drawn in a black ring on the placid water. To one side of me, the squadron of girls flew now in a circle at about the three-thousand-foot level. The platforms hovered near them.

Along the shore I could see the slow-moving line of Jim's army, crawling like a black snake over the winding, moonlit road. I had hoped that the head of it would be approaching the bluff near the west channel of the Virgins' Island. But it was not that far as yet.

I spoke into my aerial. "Make it faster, Jim! The image of him showed his smiling face. Good old Jim, always smiling. "Right," he said.

From this height there was no sign of Talon. Behind me, from Kalima, Maxite had sent out an aerial image-finder. Its pink whirling ball came sailing past me overhead.

I sat enshrouded in my black insulated suit. I switched the current into it; I could hear the current hum; smell its faint acrid odor. The apparatus of the Frazier projector was already assembled. The pulse-motor was on my wrist; the headband I now adjusted on my forehead. I made all the connections, but I did not turn on the current.

Before me were my smaller instruments. A bank of image-grids was lashed here; voice receivers were at my ears, my speaker aerial was on my shoulder. I caught the rays from the image lens mounted in Maxite's castle room. I turned into it, saw his pale, intent face, heard his grave voice.

"No sign of Talon, Leonard."

"No. I'm holding the girls and the boats ready. I'll go higher myself — your lens just passed me."

"Yes. But it shows nothing yet."

"I'll send one beyond it."

"Good luck, Leonard."

I nodded and disconnected. Sonya was calling me.

"Can't we go forward?"

"No."

From the boats down there I caught Alice's voice, but her image did not register; it was dark in the boat behind the black shields which enshrouded it.

"Len, have you seen Talon's rafts yet? Mett says he wants to know what our boats are to do?"

"Nothing. Stay as you are."

"Be . . . very careful of yourself, Leonard."

"Yes," I said. I cut off, urged my birds upward. At nearly ten thousand feet I hung poised. Far up the Warm Sea, on the west road Talon's approaching force was visible. And on the water, I saw the black blobs of his rafts, four of them, evidently huge affairs, crowded with men and apparatus. One of them was in the yellow moonlit path. I could see the swimming figures in the water, harnessed, drawing the raft slowly forward.

The pine ball I had sent out passed Maxite's. It sped toward Talon's rafts. On my grid I caught a glimpse of the wooden raft, with dead black beams standing up from it vertically in the air. Hundreds of figures crowded there. A black beam caught my whirling lens, burned it. The grid went dark.

Talon's land force was almost to the Virgins' Island channel to the north. The rafts were over near that shore. It was what I wanted to know. Talon would use the west channel.

I dropped my platform downward, and adjusted my helmet, though I kept its visor open. Talon's land force would reach the channel before mine could get there. I had hoped that Jim would be able to set up our wind projector on the bluff there to command the narrow water. But Talon would be there first unless I could halt him.

I turned to my aerial and gave the order for a general attack.

I rose again, high in the air, and urged my birds forward. Beneath me, the scene of battle spread out like a map of three dimensions. Far down, our boats showed as tiny blobs spreading through the west channel.

They were fast, but not so fast as the squadrons of flying girls.

Sonya came leading them upward. They passed me, a giant flying wedge heading over Talon's rafts. There were four rafts, three close to the shore, perhaps for protection of the land force. But one of the rafts was farther out, separated from the others. It was still several miles beyond the north tip of Virgins' Island.

Sonya's squadron was the first to make contact with the enemy. The girls headed for this isolated raft. They were ten thousand feet or more above it. My heart was heavy with apprehension. I could see the black rays from the raft standing up into the air. Would they reach that high?

It seemed not. The girls were safely over them, wheeled, and came back. They had dropped a bomb. I saw a glowing spot of light as it fell. It struck the water, wide of the raft. A surge of water mounted upward, with a spot of red light where the bomb had burst, then another, a score of them. I began to hear their sharp reports.

The raft was lashed by the waves, but still unhit. But the brutemen pulling it were disorganized, many of them killed, no doubt. The raft stopped its forward progress. Its black beam wavered, then seemed to connect into one narrow black ray.

It shot up through the girls, cut a wide swath through them. Some wavered, came fluttering down, falling, recovering, limping slowly back toward Kalima, struggling to keep above the water. Others fell like plummets into the sea. Half our girls, undoubtedly, were killed or wounded by that single black blast.

Our boats swept through the channel. Three stopped in midstream; seven surged on. Lights flared, our lurid but penetrating red flare of light went up in an arc from one of our halted boats, and burst over Talon's land force. They had spread out from the road; over by the bluff, just beyond the north end of the channel, they were erecting a huge piece of apparatus.

The light flares died. But the gunners on our three boats which had stopped in the channel had the range. I could see the streams of their electronic needles, straight paths to the shore. Dim violet beams, with white radiance where the great metallic needles were striking Talon's army.

There must have been a chaos on shore. Then from a projector there in the darkness, a great hissing rose. A yellow glow, almost like moonlight, became visible. It waved, fan-shaped from its source: a light that lingered, persisted in the darkness, spread until all along that section of the shore it hung like hovering yellow smoke, a barrage against which our electronic needles launched harmlessly. I could see them materialized into white solidity as they struck it, then flaring red, and yellow as they fused and burned.

The gunners on our boats tried curving their beams. Some were effective, curving in a great violet arc, up over the barrage, or sidewise around its edge. I judged that some were finding their mark, though the barrage was constantly shifted to check them.

The scene everywhere now was a chaos of flashing colored lights. The girls who had escaped the black blast had wavered, gone higher. Their bombs were falling wide; the sea everywhere here was lashed into foam where the bombs were bursting. A chaos of light, sound and smell: mingled electrical hums, the pungent, acrid electronic odors, the hiss of the flares, the sharp crack of the exploding bombs.

The girls for a moment withdrew, off to one side, very high up. They could not hit their marks; the black beams from the rafts, now spread purely for defense, rose cone-shaped, a cone extending widely over them to protect their swimmers. The bombs, those few that were accurately aimed, exploded in midair, as they struck the cone.

A chaos of swift, simultaneous action was everywhere taking place. Our great projectors on the flying platforms opened fire, downward at the rafts. But now from shore a solid black beam suddenly came sweeping out. It caught one of our platforms. The birds fell. The platform, its insulation inadequate, shriveled on the colorless blast, and went down, a tangled mess of birds and struggling human figures.

The beam swung. It caught another platform, and another. All six — the only six we had — were surprised by it, caught there, low over the channel, before they could escape. One by one they were crashing down into the water. The last one tried to dive; it was struck just as it neared the water level.

This black beam from Talon's shore projector was raking the channel from end to end. It seemed to have a range of several miles — a longer range than any of our weapons. It destroyed our six platforms, and then swung upward at our girls. But they were just beyond it. They wavered as they felt its effect, and then went higher and farther away.

Talon's white light flares were no continuous from shore. The scene was a dazzling glare of white, with alternating periods of blackness. The black beam, guided by the white flares, sought other victims. It swung on our boats, three of which were bombarding the shore, the other seven heading for Talon's rafts.

The three closest ones caught the black blast full. It burned through their insulating shields, as it had burned the platforms. One boat sank like a stone. Another up-ended; the third tried to retreat.

But its animals evidently were caught at the water surface and destroyed. It lay there, its needle-beam wavering. Then it, also, was hit full by the black beam. It shriveled, disappeared. The water down there was gruesome with black struggling figures.

The beam swung after our other seven boats. They were headed to attack the rafts. They felt the beam but they were farther away, and their side insulation withstood it. I roared orders at them, and by some miracle my voice got through. Alice answered me.

"Head back!" I commanded. "Around the island. Into the east channel."

It was all very swift. I had been fairly high and about a mile away when the black beam began its deadly work. It flashed by me several times, but my lone platform, with its six birds, was a small, inconspicuous object. The beam missed me; its handlers were evidently after bigger game.

In my ear Maxite's voice sounded, "Keep the girls away, Leonard! Retreat! Our land forces are too close!"

I gave the orders. Maxite's pink blobs of fire were constantly arriving from Kalima. He had seen our disaster. The black beam mounted on the shore seemed impregnable unless, perhaps from the rear, I could assault its gunners with the Frazier thought-beam. I told Maxite my plan and he approved.

I swept back toward the Virgins' Island. I would go back and come up over the west mainland, flying low. I could make such speed that in a few minutes I would be behind Talon's barrage. Talon's rafts were all well out from shore now, gathered in a group.

I swung within a mile of them. Their black, cone-shaped barrage was over them. They had made no attack, except the one upward blast at the girls, and no attack now was being made on them.

During those brief moments when we had bombed them, their swimming brutes must have suffered sever loss. Many dove, and climbed to the rafts. But some were still swimming.

The rafts were heading slowly for the north tip of the other channel.

My birds were flying with tremendous speed. Occasionally I passed wounded birds, and wounded girl riders clinging desperately to them, trying to get back to Kalima.

I sailed over the island, toward Kalima, and then turned and passed inland above the road. Jim's forces were drawn up in an arc, extending from the sea, back inland some half mile.

The heavy insulating shields were erected at intervals. The projectors were ready, and our wind projector was erected at the shore. It seemed a safe condition. Five miles or more of open country was between this line and Talon's black beam. I could see the beam from here.

But Talon's yellow shore-barrage glowed clearly. Save for that radiance, the scene up there was now dark. A lull had come to the battle. The first engagement, in which we had been so decisively worsted, was over. A momentary lull it was, while Talon seemed waiting to see what we would do next.

The scene was dark and silent. The night was darker now as

well. Black clouds obscured the Moon and all the stars to the north. And in the silence I heard a low muttering thunder.

I passed over our line, ordering Jim to remain inactive.

"Why?" he protested. "Don't I get in this at all, Len?"

But I kept him there. It was no time for us to plunge recklessly at Talon. He had surprised our first attack and worsted us in the conflict. I was not willing to try that again.

Flying low, I headed over the rolling hills for Talon's present land base. I put on my helmet, drew up the insulating shields that lined the sides of the platform. At my wrist the pulse-motor was throbbing.

I switched on the Frazier current, gripped the controls of the huge projector. If I could concentrate my thoughts enough . . . with intensity enough. I was letting them rove now, gathering strength. If I could halt that devastating black beam, and then order another attack, all our remaining forces attacking at once —

In my ears suddenly was Maxite's voice, "I'm ordering Jim to use the wind projector. Talon's forces are making for the island. We may be able to blow they away, toward the East Channel, where our boats can get at them."

Behind me I heard the hiss and roar as the great wind projector got into action, a stream of expanding, heat-yielding electrons flung in a path over the channel surface. A roar, the hot air rising, the cold wind sweeping in, the channel was soon lashed with angry waves.

It had grown very dark. Black clouds edged with lightning were coming down frm he north. The thunder claps were louder. I swung low over Talon's lines. Groups of heads clustered on the ground, some mounted on the brutemen.

A crowd moved about a huge black muzzle pointed diagonally upward toward Kalima. I passed close over it, a hundred feet up, but I hoped that for a moment I would not be seen in the darkness.

To my right was the yellow barrage radiance along the shore. Large, bowl-like wire cages set at intervals of a hundred feet. They glowed yellow, huge pots of the spreading barrage light. Mounted heads were attending them.

I dashed at one. I shouted, stood up on my swaying platform and screamed with menacing words. The heads looked up, surprised. The Frazier projector spat its intensified ray.

Woodenly, the heads and the brutemen stood stricken; the pot of light went out. I passed within fifty feet of it; my fire-flash, effective at this short range, spat its tongue of blue flame. The brutemen and the heads, the pot of barrage light itself, shriveled under the blast.

I swept along the barrage line, the Frazier beam preceding me. From the other side, and from below, yellow rings of fire darted up. They struck my upraised side-shield, and the bottom of the platform. I could hear the crack of the reports as they struck.

The encampment was in confusion, thousands of dark, surging figures. Small, black beams swung at me, mingled with the fire-rings. A light-flare burst over my head. Shouts, a rush of dim figures to avoid me; one of my birds was struck. I cut it loose. It fell.

But I was not halted; a minute or two of swift flight, the barrage went dark as I sprayed it with the Frazier beam and the blue fire. I came to the giant projector of the black ray; it shriveled, fused. Its gunners vanished under my blast.

The air was acrid with metallic gases and the smell of burning human flesh. But Talon's shoreline was dark, devastated. Another of my birds wavered; I urged them all upward. Fire-rings rocked my platform with their detonations. But I was rising. They fell away. The shouts of confusion lessened, melted beneath me.

I was over the water again, safe beyond the lines. The barrage was gone. The giant black beam was destroyed. I tried to tune in for Maxite, could not get him. But I got Jim.

"Forward! Attack now! Swiftly, Jim, with all you've got!"

Then I got Maxite. "Order the attack!"

I could not get his image. My controls were disabled, or the atmosphere was overcharged. But I heard his triumphant voice. "We'll get them, Leonard, get them now!"

The storm from the north broke with fury; no rain, but a blast of wind, sizzling lightning bolts, and the roar of thunder.

Jim had evidently abandoned his windblast. His forces were dashing forward. A spray of the violet needle beams curved up before him.

Talon's line was answering. Fire-rings were floating up. Black rays were waving. The two lines came together as Jim's army rushed forward; the rolling hills off there were a confusion of darting lights and crossing rays, myriad mid-air explosions.

Then it seemed that Talon's line was drawing back, a retreat northward. A yellow barrage went up to cover it. But Jim rushed it; the barrage vanished. With some great projector, Talon's heads made a stand.

A great ball of fire rose into the heavens, a tremendous arc over Jim's army, until it fell at the horizon. Fell on Kalima? I thought so. There was a glare against the sky over there. At five-minute intervals these fireballs went up, bombarding the distant city.

Sonya was fifteen thousand feet over the channel when our second attack began. The storm was driving the girls back; the birds could barely hold against the wind. The sea far below was a turmoil of lashing waves.

Our boats in the east channel started forward to try and reach Talon's rafts. But the rafts had blown ashore, were wrecked on the north rocky beach of the island.

Angry waves dashed over them. The heads and the brute-bodies were washed ashore with each white surge of the water.

Our boats saw it. They dropped back into the lee of the island, in the East Channel. The water was a little calmer there.

Close along the shore they hovered, and began raking the island with their needle beams, a steady outpour of violet streams, and blasts from the blue fire-guns.

The island's verdure shriveled, all along the east shore. Then Maxite ordered Jim to set a projector on the west bluff. It soon was sending a blue stream across the channel. The west side of the island was raked from end to end.

Sonya's girls were scattered by the wind. But she saw some of them poised over the north end of the island where Talon's men were trying to land from the rafts. The girls dropped a bomb, then another. The bombs were finding their marks.

Sonya urged her birds in that direction. But abruptly the thought of Altho came clear and vivid to her mind. She had long since given Altho up for dead, killed by our own weapons. But he was not dead. His thoughts came to her with sudden clearness.

I saw the bombardment of Kalima finally halted. Jim, victorious, was sweeping everything before him. His projector still raked the island. The island's vegetation was burning now from end to end. On the north beach the huddled figures were nearly gone; bodies were everywhere. The water was dotted with them.

Along the main shore now, in advance of Jim, Talon's army was in utter rout. Frantic brutemen with mounted heads rushed to the beach, plunged in. The heads were torn away, floating like balloons on the white lashing waves. Back along the shore, Jim's men were lined. Needle beams darted out at the floating heads.

Everywhere we were winning. Far back in the country I could see Jim's triumphant lights, spreading everywhere.

From the turmoil of water beneath me, a boat rose up, a long, narrow black boat. Its cover slid back. It was heading northward, away from Kalima, speeding swiftly, with a line of bubbles in its wake.

I remembered it; the boat Jim had described. Talon's boat! Talon, who had been lurking beneath the surface of the sea, waiting in safety for victory, so that he might rush for Kalima. Now, with defeat, he was escaping. Altho, perhaps, was with him.

I turned my aerial, trying to pick up Maxite. But I could not get him. Then I tried one of our nearest boats raking the island, ordered it to follow Talon. Behind me, far down, I saw it turn and start.

I drove my birds downward in a swoop for Talon's boat. Beneath me, close to the water I seemed to see the shadow of a flying bird, but in a moment I had forgotten it.

A breathless swoop and I was close upon the boat. From the dim glow of its engines, I saw it held only four figures, three mounted heads. Two were controlling the boat. The other was Talon. I could see him moving about giving commands. And Altho lay in the boat's bottom, Altho, his body lashed and bound into an inert bundle.

My Frazier beam struck the boat's interior. The two mounted heads controlling it stiffened and fell. But Talon was untouched. I was close over the stern of the boat, holding my projector downward. Talon's face glared up at me, untouched. His brute-body stiffened and slumped, but Talon disconnected from it.

His head dropped to the deck upon his hands. His eyes glared up at me. A flash of black spat from his hand-projector. At this close range my platform crumbled. It fell, struck the boat's stern, and toppled half into the water. I had leaped. I fell into the boat.

But another figure had landed there before me, a giant, fluttering bird. Sonya jumped from it, seized Altho's bound body. Talon's small flash darted at her, but missed.

My wrecked platform, half on the boat's stern, weighed it down. The boat began to fill with water.

I saw vaguely as I leaped at Talon, that Sonya was dragging Altho's inert form to the gunwale. They went overboard together. My hurtling body struck the head of Talon. It cracked, smashed under my weight. I climbed from its noisome, sticky mass.

The boat was filling, sinking stern first. I dove over its side, into the wave-whipped sea.

The sinking boat sucked me under. But I came up. Around me was a white, tumultuous darkness. Overhead the storm clouds had broken into a rift; the yellow moonlight came through. Something was floating near me, some wreckage from the boat, a gas-filled pontoon. I seized it.

Behind me, our boat from the island was approaching. Then I saw, upraised near me by a surging wave-crest, a human figure struggling. Sonya, struggling to keep Altho above the water. I reached them.

"Sonya! Here, hold to this! I've got him!"

A sea animal went by us with a rush. Our pursuing boat drew up; its black side was a wall above us. The insulating side-shield rolled back. Anxious men's faces stared down at us over the gunwale. Arms came down and hauled us up.

I heard Alice's voice; and Dolores's. "Len! And Sonya . . . and the prince! Thank God you're all safe!"

And from far over the land came the scream of Jim's siren, the signal of victory there.

XVIII

THE GREAT RIDDLE

THE HOMECOMING! The return of our war-racked forces to the city, with half its suburbs burned, and a thousand of its people killed by Talon's bombardment! I shall not describe the cheers, the laughter, the sobbing. Victory in war can seem to be so little better than defeat! All the paeans of triumph cannot heal the maimed, or bring back the dead.

I was king no longer, for our prince now was ruler, with Sonya for his queen. I was glad to be released. There is a very false, a pseudo-glory, in ruling a nation.

But Altho would not have me wholly resign. My promised reforms, my Earthly ideas of government, were needed here. And so they called me premier, and thrived upon a crude but humane version of what we on Earth would call a civilized government: a veneration of the aged, a new idea of infant welfare, a monogamy of marriage with the surplus women doing their rational work in art and industry.

Of Talon's thousand, fully half of them escaped back into the mountains. They are there now. They will always be a menace. But there is not a race of humans in all the universe unmenaced by something. The very essence of human existence is struggle. We do not think of Talon's brutes now as the Nameless Horror, and we are always prepared.

It was shortly after my marriage to Alice, that one evening I came upon Jim and Dolores in each other's arms.

"Well!" I said. "What's this?"

He kissed her again. "I loved her right from the beginning," he declared.

Which was not exactly true, but I knew he thought so.

I had never seen little Dolores so radiant. "And I always loved him, Len. You know that."

I did indeed. And she had never wavered in that love, from the day when he had seized the little blind child and whirled her in the air.

Our return to Earth? We never made it. With Dr. Weatherby's death, the grave held the vital knowledge we needed for such a journey. Nor did we desire it. Our lives were cast here.

Often now, from Earth, thought-waves reach me, tiny Earth, rolling on with a speeding time so much faster than ours in this outer realm! Centuries have passed on Earth. Of what use for me to return — a primitive, savage being of their past ages?

Civilizations have risen, held their peak, and declined. Great cities have come and gone. Ice has been again where once I saw the jungles of the tropics. And the ice has melted again through countless ages.

The new humans of Earth often communicate with me. Their thoughts are amazed at what I have to tell them. It is all amazing to me, the great riddle of the universe. And I think sometimes of that ancient Earth-astronomer, groping with the riddle, writing in his ancient book:

Man, the little god of this Earth, tied down to the small star which infinite Nature gave him for an abode, storms forth into immeasurable stellar space with his thoughts.

From that little Earth I stormed forth in body, beyond the stars!

THE END

www.ingramcontent.com/pod-product-compliance
Lightning Source LLC
Chambersburg PA
CBHW051254170626
46809CB00004B/1650